THE LIFE CYCLE

The Life Cycle

by

Paul Kane

BLACK SHUCK
SHADOWS

Black Shuck Books
www.BlackShuckBooks.co.uk

All stories © Paul Kane
Nightlife © 2002
Half-Life © 2011
Lifetime © 2015
Another Life © 2017

Cover design & internal layout © Great British Horror 2018

The right of Paul Kane to be identified as the author of this work has been asserted by him in accordance with the Copyright, Designs & Patents Act 1988.
All rights reserved. This book is sold subject to the condition that it shall not be reproduced in whole or in part, in any form or by any means, electronic or mechanical, including photocopying, recording, or by any information storage and retrieval system now known of hereafter invented, without written permission from the publisher and without a similar condition, including this condition, being imposed on the subsequent purchaser.

First published in the UK by Black Shuck Books, 2017

978-1979170390

7
Nightlife

21
Half-Life

95
Lifetime

169
Another Life

203
Story Notes

Nightlife

There's nothing like a good night out.

And in his mind, Neil was already there. He wasn't standing behind this counter, stamping books one after the other. Taking them from people as they ambled in through the heavy wooden doors.

'Next please. Oh, I'm afraid there's a fine to pay on this one, sir.'

It was all done on automatic pilot, because he was dreaming of the pleasures to come in just a few short hours. It seemed like ages since he'd gone out and enjoyed himself, but it couldn't have been so long ago. Besides, he knew it was that much better when he got together with the guys rather than tearing off on his own. That meant waiting for everyone to be free at the same time. Waiting for the *right* time.

That was what made it such a big deal, he

supposed, meeting up with his old university pals every few weeks. It was something to look forward to, and he definitely intended to make the most of it. Anyway, they were all older than they used to be when they started this game – well, twenty-seven wasn't young by today's standards. And they could only realistically manage this sort of thing every so often.

It was a real physical effort staying out most of the night, and in the morning you felt like you'd been run over by a truck. Neil's muscles always ached, his stomach begged him never to eat or drink again, and his head usually felt like someone was trying to crack it open with a pickaxe. He needed a little time to recuperate, ready for the next outing. But Neil knew it was all worthwhile. One day he'd look back on these memories, on the last few years, with a nostalgic fondness and wish he could still do the things he'd do tonight. Life's too short for regrets.

Neil slotted the next borrower card into the scanner and passed through a fresh batch of books, without looking at the titles once. His thoughts were elsewhere. He was planning what they would get up to based on their previous adventures. Him, Adrian, Ryan, Owen, Luke and Jack. God, what a motley gang of misfits. He couldn't even remember how they'd all hooked up together at uni, so many moons ago now. It wasn't as if they'd been taking the same subjects or anything. Neil just figured they'd tracked each other down: the party animals. Kindred spirits with similar interests and goals, who could usually be found propping up the bar at the Student's Union between seminars.

Like him, they'd all chosen this particular city for its nightlife, as opposed to the academic opportunities it could offer them. What was the point of thinking about crap like that anyway? It was virtually impossible to find the job you wanted nowadays, even *with* qualifications. Owen and Ryan were still signing on to this day, having only briefly dabbled in the work market.

But yeah, this place was buzzing on a Friday and Saturday night. Actually, the city was buzzing on any night you cared to venture out. Only the weekend jaunt was a kind of special thing. Plus you had all day Sunday to rest up, or at least try to.

At any given time there would be dozens and dozens of people in the streets and down back alleys, on their way to pubs, nightclubs, hotels; anywhere they could have a good time and forget about the drudgery of their everyday lives. The sights, the sounds, the smells. There was something in the air at night that would be well and truly gone by the next day. Something that drove grown men wild with desire…and sometimes drove women even wilder! What was it they called it in that film with Travolta? A fever. Yes, it was a kind of fever that gripped them, turning the city into a hotbed of lust, debauchery and depravity. Come eight or nine o'clock that night he'd be out there in the thick of it all. Neil couldn't wait.

He knew the routine by now. Soon as his shift ended and he'd helped tidy up at the library, he'd hurry back to his tiny flat to get ready. Preparation was everything. First he'd shower, washing off the grime of the day. Then he'd spruce himself up a bit, clean his teeth and change into something more comfortable. Something more appropriate. Like a thousand times before, Neil was hoping he'd get lucky while he was out on the pull.

On the last occasion they'd all gone out together, Luke had scored with a real dish. He'd been eyeing her up all evening, and Neil could hardly blame him. Five-foot-nine, redhead with a gorgeous body, all poured into a slinky satin dress which left very little to the imagination.

Finally, he'd approached her, and from that moment on she hadn't really stood a chance. Luke could be very persuasive, and he wasn't exactly ugly himself (Neil didn't think so, at any rate; none of the women he'd ever gone after could resist his charms). The rest of them had remained on the sidelines as he made his final play, watching jealously as she fell for him.

Luke later told him that they'd done the business in a backstreet behind the club where he'd first spotted her. Neil could see it in his imagination: Luke clawing at the silky material of that dress, the young girl squirming beneath his touch, the sensation of Luke's tongue running over her face, her breasts...and lower still.

Hungry for her.

Maybe Neil would find someone like that

tonight instead of the typical dregs he was used to. The thought aroused him and he fought to control himself.

A middle-aged woman wearing glasses was looking at him strangely over the counter. What was she taking out? Mmm... Love stories, thrillers. *Sad.* Some people just didn't know how to live life. All they could do was fantasise. Read about it and wish, and wish...

When Neil gazed into her eyes he could tell there was nothing going on behind them. He could sense it. If she'd only seen a tenth of the things he'd seen in the years since his eighteenth birthday...

She'd probably been saddled with a family by the time she was his age, married by twenty-one, frightened of being left on the shelf. And now, a couple of decades later, the kids had flown the coop – Neil probably even saw them when he was out and about round the city. Leaving her with nothing but an empty house and a husband who barely spoke to her anymore.

How did he know all these things? Because she was just like his own mother. This poor woman's life was exactly the same as that of his parents. Safe. Comfortable. *Boring.* It wasn't their fault. That's all they'd ever known, all they'd ever been: restricted, repressed.

They'd never had the same opportunities as him. His parents hadn't enjoyed the same kind of freedom Neil took for granted now, living in that quiet country village. Small community, people watching their every move. They had to be so very careful.

Neil didn't intend to live his life like that, following in their footsteps. Suppressing his emotions and longings. That's why he'd left home as soon as he could, come here to be with people of his own age, his own inclination. The world had moved on. It was no longer a sin to indulge yourself. But Neil's folks were so out of touch, they could never understand. The generation gap strikes again.

He handed the books back over to the woman, having dated them inside. One month from today.

'T—Thank you,' she said, taking them from him, a little unsure of herself. Was it suddenly hot in the library? And was her pulse-rate suddenly up? Heart pounding?

Neil chuckled to himself as she backed out

through the door, glancing at the odd librarian who'd stared so intently at her.

Now where had he been? Oh yes, running through what would happen when he left the flat.

He'd meet up with the rest of them at the usual place, a park just off Milton Street. From here they'd make their way into the city itself. It wasn't far for them. No real need for taxis or busses. In fact it was probably faster on foot.

The closer they came to the action, the more they would eat and drink, stopping off along the way for swift ones. They had to keep up their strength for the marathon ahead of them. Come to think of it, the journey in was probably the best part. Messing about with the guys, playful backbiting and mock fights.

But in all this time Neil and the others had never once come across any real trouble.

He'd heard the stories, of course he had. Of people being beaten up, noses broken. Maybe even the flash of steel as things got out of hand, probably over a girl or a spilt drink. There were some who even went out with the express intention of causing bother. Nutters cropped up everywhere these days. You couldn't get away from that awful fact. It was a dangerous world.

Thankfully, they'd managed to avoid any fracas of this nature directly. Neil couldn't explain it. Perhaps there was safety in numbers, for they tended to stick together most of the night – unless one of them was…otherwise engaged, as Luke had been the other week; but even then the missing member would always return to the fold soon after. Or was it the fact that they gave off certain signals to would-be aggressors? Warning signs.

But no doubt about it, Neil had to conclude that it was more the anticipation, the excitement of approaching the city centre that really did it for him. Such a choice of things to do, new people to meet.

And not for the first time his eyes found their way up to the clock over those varnished doors. It was taunting him, winding down, dragging out the last excruciating half-hour before they closed to the general public. Only then could he begin to clear up: collecting discarded books together and placing them on the trolley ready for re-shelving, cashing up (it was surprising how much they made from fines, and then there was the photocopier to consider), and so on and so forth. He'd probably skip through a lot of this today so he could get off a bit earlier.

Neil wasn't alone, though. He had a good idea what was occupying the thoughts of his friends. They'd be just as eager as he was for night to come, so they could let their collective hair down. He could picture Adrian now, pacing up and down at the burger bar where he worked, serving those terrible greasy meals with meat that had no distinguishing flavour to it – who could eat that foul grill-cooked shite? Luke would probably be arriving back from his travels in his capacity as a rep; he really did have the heart and soul of a gypsy, that one. Jack would be rehearsing with his heavy metal band, Brutal ('We'll make it big some day,' he was always telling them. To be fair they weren't half bad)… And as for Ryan and Owen, well they'd probably just be getting out of their pits around now and having a spot of 'breakfast'. All right for some!

But no matter what they were doing, all of them would have one eye on a clock or a watch, counting down the minutes, the hours, until they could come together once more.

*

Finally, at last, the endless torture was just about over and an impatient Neil was away. He sprinted to his car, a feeling of tremendous excitement alive inside of him. Like a child on Christmas Eve, it wouldn't be long now before he could open his presents.

And stepping out of the shower back home, he let the water drip from his taut physique. Neil didn't bother to shave; there was no point, really. Instead, he started towelling himself off and walked into the living room.

Neil went over to the window, opened it. The night was already drawing in. On the horizon a powerless sun was dying, taking with it the last vestiges of daylight. But there was another source ready and willing to take its place. Hanging over the city, irradiating the buildings, the streets he would be exploring later. Bathing everything in a haunted silvery sheen.

He stood naked at the window and listened to the sounds of night-time assaulting his ears. Raised voices, TVs, music, sirens…and something else. A rhythmic throbbing.

Thousands of heartbeats all pumping as one.

The life-force of the city.

From his vantage point several floors above ground level, he could see the sights. Weird neon signs cranking up – Harry's, Monty's, The Green Room. Places he knew intimately. Inside and out.

Now he closed his eyes, the towel dropping out of his hands. Neil sniffed at the cool night air streaming in. He could smell them. The time was nearly upon him. He had waited quite long enough.

When he opened his eyes again the sky was full of stars, and a familiar white shape rolled out from behind the cover of grey-blue clouds.

Neil could feel the adrenaline rushing through him. This time he didn't hold back. Soon it would begin. He could already feel the tingling as new hairs appeared all over his body, as his eyes took on a frightening yellow and red cast.

Then, when it was over, when he was totally free again, he would climb down and hunt with the pack. With his brothers. Seeking their quarry. No one would miss a few; the supply was plentiful in the city.

A lengthy tongue brushed over teeth that were pointed and gleaming, that could bite through anything. He could almost taste the flesh. Almost savour the flowing blood.

Illuminated by the full moon, Neil smiled.

No, there's nothing like a good night out, he thought. Nothing like it in the world.

Half-Life

As Neil sat staring at the entrance, nursing his pint of bitter, he thought about the past.

How could he not, today of all days? His eyes flitted from the doorway of the Royal Oak pub to the dirty brown liquid in the glass below, to the handful of other patrons this Friday evening. There weren't many: a sweaty looking man with a skin complaint, red blotches splattering his cheeks and nose; a sad-looking couple in their 50s who weren't speaking to each other; a twenty-something in a hoodie playing the fruit machine, obviously biding his time before meeting up with mates or heading out on the town later.

It's what he would have been doing sixteen-odd years ago, and even before that. Neil remembered those nights, getting ready to go on the prowl, hitting the nightclubs in the wilder parts of the city with the pack. Picking up the ladies then doing all sorts with them, usually in the alleyways behind the clubs…

He'd always promised himself those days would carry on forever, that he wouldn't get old – and at forty-three (alright, almost forty-four), was he really that ancient? Enough to be the oldest swinger in town if he went there now on a Friday night. He'd stand out like a sore thumb against the teens and the tweens, the loud techno beats more likely to give him a headache nowadays than get his adrenalin pumping.

The fact that he was here, in a pub outside of town itself, for a gathering that would only make him feel even more depressed about the turns his life had taken, wasn't helping. His focus shifted from the booze to his belly, not massive by any means, but not a patch on the flat washboard stomach he'd had back then. He kept telling himself that he could get back into shape anytime he wanted, but never did. Didn't really care or want to, if the truth be known.

What the hell was wrong with him? When had all this apathy begun?

Might've been when you settled down and embraced the life of a stay-at-home miserable bastard, he said to himself and couldn't help a tired laugh. That had been his parents' existence: safe, comfortable, not taking any risks – *ever*. Stick-in-the-muds that he couldn't wait to get away from when he was younger, always telling himself he wouldn't turn out like them; wouldn't just piss his life away sitting in of an evening watching TV. He'd wanted to get out there, experience life at the sharp end – and he'd done just that...for a while. But it seemed he had more in common with them than he realised, even though he'd later discovered that he was in fact adopted. Made sense when you thought about it, given his...affliction (curse, whatever you wanted to call it). Neither his mum nor dad even hinted at anything like that, would've died rather than let themselves be taken over by their baser desires. Which meant that he'd got this from his genes, from one or both of his *real* parents. Neil sometimes thought about tracking them down, but again, he just couldn't be bothered. They probably wouldn't want to see him anyway, the runt of whatever horrible litter they'd created. They wouldn't have given Neil up in the first place if they'd thought anything of him.

The door opened and he looked up sharply, sniffing the air. His reflexes were still pretty good, and he knew even before the person walked in that it wasn't anybody he was expecting. *Just an old man in a raincoat who stank of piss, looking for company on another lonely evening.*

Neil's thoughts turned again to the past and its impact on the present.

He wondered, once more, what the others would be like when he saw them again. His old mates that he'd hooked up with at university, a gang that had found each other and then been practically inseparable for so long. Up until he was almost thirty, they'd all be going out together on the lash every few weeks…when the time was right. He'd enjoyed those adventures so much, from his late teens until—

Right, you enjoyed those times so much that you turned your back on them. Turned your back on your best friends.

That wasn't true; he hadn't turned his back

on anyone. He'd just changed. They all had. For one thing Jack was starting to make headway with his band, Brutal, which one review described as 'the rock equivalent of being given a blow-job backstage at a lingerie fashion shoot'. Before too long he was talking about albums and tours, then all of a sudden he was gone. Adrian had worked his way up from serving in a burger bar to being the manager, moving to where the head office was, while model-look-a-like Luke's repping took him further and further afield, with no one real place he could call his home anymore. As for Owen and Ryan, they'd eventually got their act together enough to get off the dole (helped by the fact that the benefits system was undergoing an overhaul and anyone who didn't at least attempt to find work had their money cut). Owen had actually joined the police force, if you could believe it; was doing pretty well by all accounts, but had moved several times with his job. Ryan had attempted to hold down one job after another, from builder's apprentice – in spite of his age – to night watchman (that was a good one). Last Neil heard, he was doing manual labour on a farm – better lock up those chickens – but he was the only one of the group who'd remained relatively local (well, within fifty miles, anyway – but it was surprising how far that distance was when you really didn't *want* to see someone). The most local apart from Neil, that was, who hadn't moved at all – except to another, quieter, part of town. Out of his flat and into somewhere bigger. With:

Julie.

She'd come along even before Jack went off with the band, though, hadn't she? The more he thought about it, the more Neil wondered whether he had been the catalyst for them *all* breaking up and going their separate ways. He hadn't been their ring leader by any means – had there even been such a thing? – but maybe he'd been the glue that bound them all together. He hadn't thought of himself as such, but the guys *had* sort of gravitated towards him at uni, been drawn into his orbit one by one. Neil had always thought of Luke, or perhaps Jack, as the dominant force in their rag-tag bunch, but once he'd taken himself out of the equation things *had* fallen apart pretty quickly. And he'd taken himself out of the equation because of:

Julie.

It all came back to her, didn't it? If he hadn't met her, then maybe—

Neil shook his head and took another sip of his bitter. He loved Julie (loved as in past tense? or present?). She hadn't been like the rest; not one of the women he and his mates targeted on their nights out, Luke usually getting to the most attractive ones first, although Neil hadn't done so badly in his time. This had been different. For one thing, he'd met her outside of the group – when he was doing a grocery shop, in fact. He'd been wandering about in the supermarket with his basket, head up his arse, thinking about the approaching fun that coming Friday (back then it had been the highlight of his month). He'd turned the corner and almost knocked her over. As it was he'd knocked the basket out of her hands.

'Why don't you watch where you're going?' she'd said.

'I'm really sorry,' he'd replied, stooping to pick up her microwave meals for one, tins of soup and assorted fruit and vegetables. But he couldn't take his eyes off her face. Even in all the times he'd been out with the lads, he'd never seen anyone as pretty as her: short, strawberry-blonde hair, cropped so that it framed her face then hung in bangs just under her chin; the most piercing green eyes, like sapphires shining out of a mine; and those lips, the fullest you could ever imagine. She didn't need any lipstick, any make-up, and it was a good job too because she hadn't bothered for this trip to the store. Nor had she dressed up: she was just wearing jeans and a jumper, with a short denim jacket – well, she hadn't been expecting to bump into the soon-to-be love of her life.

However, the overall effect of her appearance on Neil had been nothing short of revelatory.

(Later, when the other members of the circle had seen her, they'd said she was nothing special – that he was deluding himself. Neil knew different, knew that they were only jealous; that he had something as magnificent as Julie and they didn't. Later, much later, he began to see what they meant...)

'I should think *so*,' she said, taking the basket from him. Their fingers had touched, and she'd felt the spark. Neil had made sure of that. It was one of the perks of being who he was – *what* he was. He'd looked into those green eyes, in a bid to entrance her as much as she'd entranced him. And…there it was. Her heart was beating just a little quicker, not a consequence of banging into him, almost falling, but something else. The effect he was purposefully having on her. Provoking feelings in her that he knew were already bubbling away beneath the surface. She'd been alone long enough, he felt it, could smell it – the consequence of being hurt by a man in the past. Time to change all that, time she had someone. Someone like Neil. 'Listen,' she said, suddenly smiling, her breathing fast and shallow, 'I know it sounds crazy but…do you want to get out of here? Maybe go somewhere?'

He nodded. 'I thought you'd never ask.'

In those early days when they looked back and chatted about the time they'd met, Julie would mention how they'd just clicked, how something had told her it was the right thing to do: to go with him right there and then, back to his flat. 'I just couldn't help myself,' she'd say, giggling. Little realising that she'd had a 'push'. That he'd done the same kind of number on her he had to all those others, the same thing Luke and the rest had pulled to get those girls in those nightclubs outside into the alleys. No – he told himself, and would *keep* telling himself – it was what Julie had wanted. It hadn't been the same.

Ten minutes later, the shopping was forgotten and they were back at his place, all over each other. It was animalistic, that first time – and many times after that. They were tearing off each other's clothes, raking each other's skin; biting, sucking, rutting on his bed. They'd done it five times that evening, Neil barely pausing for breath between sessions (he'd excelled himself, even he had to admit, spurred on by Julie's beauty, the magnificence of her body – it had been a long time since he'd thought of it like that – the scent of her). Afterwards, they'd lain on the bed, puffing, sweaty and exhausted. And Neil had held her, cradling her in his arms – thankful that it was only close to that time of the month rather than into it. Not hers, but his...

They both had work the next day, Julie explaining that she was a primary school teacher, Neil revealing he was a librarian, but it had been hard parting. She wanted to see him again that weekend, but he reluctantly had to confess he had plans. 'I always see my old uni mates round about now,' he explained – badly. 'They'd be upset if I cried off.'

Julie's face had fallen. 'Fine! If you don't want to see me, just say so.'

Neil had cupped that face in his hand, then said: 'I'm not like him.'

Julie frowned. 'Who?'

He realised he'd said too much, given away what he'd sensed about her, smelled on her – just one of those extra abilities that came with the territory, a kind of magic (though far stronger when it was almost that 'special time'). 'Erm, whoever it was that hurt you,' he told her. 'I won't ever do that.' It seemed a strange thing to say to someone you'd left angry red scratches all over the previous night, but he knew what he meant. Thankfully, so did Julie.

'No, I don't believe you would, Neil.' They'd agreed to meet up the following Monday, and those three days were probably the worst he'd ever spent. The guys knew there was something wrong, but hadn't been able to put their finger on it; he'd masked Julie's scent pretty well and none of them had ever been able to read him. It had just been the way he'd hung back as the others checked out what was on offer in places like Monty's and The Green Room – 'Quite a bit of talent out there,' Adrian had said, that cheeky grin plastered on his face. He'd nudged Neil, but got no response. 'What's the fuck's the matter with you?'

'Nothing,' Neil lied.

And he'd taken part, reluctantly, in the proceedings – which on the Saturday night had included luring a trio of girls outside so they could have their way with them. Neil remembered it well, even after he *changed*. It wasn't like the movies, wasn't what people thought. Yes, it was the full moon that weekend, but that didn't mean you instantly turned. It was brought on by what they were doing out there with those girls, brought on by the taste of blood and flesh. If you didn't do it voluntarily, then that was a different matter – the beast inside would usually break out at some point, take over. It was better to be in control, to satisfy the hunger like this than drive yourself into a rampage. Besides, it was fun. Or at least it had been, before:

Julie.

Neil had been the last one to transform in that alleyway. All he could see when Luke, Owen, Ryan, Jack and Aide were taking their turn with the girls was Julie's face. Julie's face instead of the brunette that Ryan was tearing into, ripping a piece out of her neck, while Jack took chunks out of her thigh; Julie's face instead of the young blonde girl being held with arms outstretched, Adrian and Owen sinking their teeth into one limb each; Julie's face instead of the tanned girl with the short skirt that Luke was slavering over, tongue descending, forcing her legs apart and then claiming a lump of her most sensitive parts, which he swallowed greedily. As busy as they were, they all took a moment to look back at him, wondering why he wasn't joining them in this feast. Swallowing, Neil brought on the wolf – his eyes taking on that terrifying yellow and red cast, hairs sprouting as his jaw elongated, slipping out of his clothes momentarily so they didn't get covered in blood.

He'd joined them, but again hung back – only lapping at the pools of scarlet liquid, which appeared black in the moonlight, giving it the sheen of motor oil. The taste of it should have sent him wild; but it didn't, not tonight. Once he'd longed for girls like these to ravage, to devour, but now he felt disgusted. *Disgusting.*

When it was all over, and the clean-up done – including morphing back into human form – the group took him to one side. 'Okay,' said Luke, lighting up a cigarette (he always smoked after feeding), 'give.'

'Yeah,' said Jack, scratching his beard, the tattoos on his hand and lower arm clearly visible, 'what's the problem, Neilly-boy? Not getting past it, are you?' He laughed and Neil remembered that sound now, because it had meant to be ironic. These days it certainly had more resonance.

Past it.

'Nothing...nothing's wrong,' he'd said again and they could at least sense that it was. He wasn't a good enough actor to fool them for long. Nevertheless, they hadn't got it out of him that night, nor the next. In fact, it only came to light when Owen and Ryan had spotted him out on a date with Julie a couple of weeks later, coming out of the cinema holding hands.

That had led to what Adrian had called an 'intervention'. They'd all been waiting for him one night after work, bundled him into the back of Jack's van, and questioned, tried to fathom out exactly what he was playing at.

'I'm not playing at *anything*,' he'd told them. 'I think…I think she's the one.'

'The one what?' asked Aide.

'There aren't any "ones",' Jack spat. 'Only the next meal.'

Ryan looked at him seriously. 'You do know you can't have a normal life with this woman, don't you? How can you?'

Neil had shrugged. He hadn't really thought that far ahead, to be honest. But he didn't want to hear it from them, didn't want to admit it right there and then (he was ready to admit it now, though, all these years later…*oh yes*).

'Why don't you do yourself a favour and leave her to us, we'll take care of the problem,' Ryan had told him, pushing his greasy hair back out of his eyes. 'We'll make it quick, this full moon coming. You can watch if you like. Might even fancy her more when we've...made a few improvements.' He'd raked the air with his nails and that had been it. Neil had leapt forward, grabbing him and slamming him against the wall of the van. It had taken Luke, Jack *and* Adrian to pull him off.

'You touch her,' he'd snarled. 'Any of you fucking so much as look at her...' He hadn't finished that sentence; hadn't needed to.

They'd let him go, all gaping at each other like they'd just been slapped in the face. Then seeing the look in his eye, and knowing he meant business. That had been the moment, the pivotal moment – and he'd felt dreadful afterwards. The lads had dropped him off with promises that they'd talk about this some other time, but gradually – and inevitably – he'd lost contact with them. He certainly hadn't joined them on their monthly nights out anymore; couldn't, after what had happened on the last occasion. Neil began spending more and more time with Julie, until they were almost inseparable. It wasn't as hard as he thought it might be, controlling those urges – even on the three nights when they were at their height. Neil found that if he fed privately just before the evening, stealing what he needed from the local abattoir, it was easier to dull the ache he felt by not running with the pack. If it got too much for him, when he thought he might hurt Julie inadvertently, he'd make up some excuse to be away for a couple of nights – usually work-related. She bought it, after all they spent the rest of the month together, and they were happy.

When his friends drifted off in their own directions, he'd clung more and more to Julie. So much so that it seemed like the logical thing for them to get married. They were a partnership now, the two of them against the world. It would mean giving up his bachelor pad, mean them pooling their resources and putting down a deposit on a house in the 'burbs, but it would be worth it to be so close. Julie, thankfully, didn't have many relatives or friends. Neil had even less, and had no intentions of inviting his pretend parents to the small affair. They spent the money they'd saved on a nice honeymoon instead, one of the best periods of Neil's life.

It was after that things started to fall apart. Julie began talking about a family and, though he hadn't thought about it before, Neil began to warm to the idea. Looking back, he couldn't believe what he'd been thinking. If he'd inherited his traits from his real parents – or one of them – then wouldn't he run the risk of passing this on to his son or daughter? In the end it turned out not to be an issue, because after trying for a while they were both tested and it was found that the chances of Julie ever conceiving were slim to negligible; some kind of problem with her ovulation. Again, that time of the month – just hers this time.

Whether she felt like she'd failed, Neil wasn't sure, or that he'd look elsewhere for the mother of his children (he wouldn't), but that's when things began to grow distant between them. They even ended up having a row one night when she mentioned the possibility of adopting. Neil told her why he was against it, but she just hadn't been able to understand.

'I don't see what one has to do with the other. You had a decent upbringing because of being adopted, didn't you?'

Neil couldn't deny it; his parents had done a good job of looking after him. It was just that it had all been a lie, and he'd come from somewhere else. Was some*thing* else, but Neil wasn't ready to share that particular fact with Julie, even then. She'd ended up shouting, he'd shouted back – the kind of passion they'd used to experience in the bedroom. Then he'd stormed out, going to get drunk in the Oak – which was rapidly becoming his bolt-hole away from everything. It was peaceful at least, and nobody really disturbed him.

When he returned that night, more a little worse for wear, she'd said nothing – just sat there on the couch with her arms folded, watching some old black and white film, but not really taking it in. They barely exchanged a word, even as they got ready for bed, and then into the next day. Then the day after that...

It became the norm that they'd hardly talk, the lack of communication turning into a comfortable habit. It seemed a better alternative to the bickering that would flare up over nothing. They'd work, come home, watch television then go to bed, usually curled up on their own side – the divide between them more than just distance. Neil knew that she still loved him, and he loved her – but something had broken fundamentally and he didn't know how to fix it.

Probably wasn't a coincidence that at the same time this was happening, Neil began to feel his baser urges increasing. Sometimes it was all he could do to keep from transforming right there and then of an evening, if it was full moon. The bloody raw meat he managed to get his hands on was no longer cutting it for him, and he began to think more and more about the past, about his time with the other members of the gang. That just made things worse. Sometimes, to his shame, he'd think about those girls and *give* them Julie's face, but it would actually make him more stimulated. Neil had taken to retreating to a safe place during those three nights every month, locking himself up in the basement of the library. There was a barred cubby hole meant for keeping the rarest books safe from burglars, but it also served to keep Neil *in*. It was no way to live, he realised that, but wasn't sure what he could do about the situation. Julie accepted whatever excuse he gave, usually without question – but the odd sideways look and bite of the lip told him that she thought he was seeing another woman. She never questioned him about it openly. Probably frightened of the answer.

Those days were gone, though. The days when Neil would 'see' lots of women. They were gone and he'd never be able to get them back. For one thing, his mates were God knows where.

Which was why it had been such a surprise when he received Owen's email at the library. He'd read it with his mouth open, especially when it said he was getting everyone back together again – and they were going to meet in their old stomping ground. His town. Neil had been excited and nervous at the same time. He'd been tempted to answer immediately, but held off for half a day because he didn't want to appear desperate. Then he'd said it'd be great to catch up, and he'd suggested the Oak as a meeting place, hoping it wouldn't be too tame. No, it wasn't – but Owen wanted them all to get together as soon as possible. Neil had told Julie the truth for a change, that he was hooking up with the old buddies he'd had when she came along (and had chosen her over). She'd looked at him and shrugged, but then enquired as to whether there would be any women there. Neil had shrugged back – there might be, in the pub itself; it was a free country. She'd told him to be back early and he'd nodded, sighing.

So now he was here, waiting. Looking up every time he heard the door go – every time he heard a noise. Neil couldn't believe they were all going to be back together again, the first time in so long. Maybe now he could get a few things off his chest, including the fact he was sorry for the way he'd acted. The way he'd ruined everything – and wished that they could get it back, though he knew that wasn't possible.

Just age talking (past it), age and regret. You reap what you sow, Neil... Reap what you—

Suddenly they were here, or at least one of them was. The door swung inwards to reveal Luke. He'd got older, but still had his good looks – the ones that would've helped him sell vodka to the Russians if he had a mind to. Nevertheless, he *had* aged. He was becoming what some women might call distinguished-looking. Neil rose, not sure what to do or say, but luckily Luke did it for him, walking over and giving him a big hug.

'It's good to see you, man,' said his friend, clapping him on the shoulder. 'You haven't changed a bit.' Then Neil caught him looking down at the beer belly. 'Well, maybe just a little.' By way of contrast, Luke had kept himself in good shape – but then he'd always boasted one of those metabolisms that ran so fast food and drink passed through him almost without being digested. (He'd also quit smoking; Neil could smell it…or, more accurately, couldn't.)

Neil found himself smiling, in spite of the ribbing. He was very glad to see his friend again and offered to buy him a drink. Luke waved him down. 'I'll sort it out. And what about you, what's that you're drinking? Bitter? What happened to the lager freak we all knew and loved? All right, bitter it is then.'

Neil thought about it, then shook his head. 'I'll just have a Diet Coke.'

'Oh come on,' said Luke. 'I was only joking. You'll have something stronger, surely?'

'I'll wait till the others get here,' he told him. 'Look, now you've arrived, any idea what brought all this on…? I mean, don't get me wrong, it's great to see you after…' Neil paused, then aborted the sentence completely. 'But why now?'

'I'm as puzzled as you are,' admitted Luke, 'Owen didn't say very much to me at all.' He went over to the bar, and by the time he'd bought the round – Neil's coke and a Bacardi for himself – Owen had arrived.

There was an air about him Neil hadn't seen before, one of authority that his years in the force had obviously granted him. Unlike Luke, Owen *wasn't* smiling. He looked more serious than Neil had ever seen him, though admittedly he was used to the carefree-dole-layabout Owen rather than the copper. Owen might as well have had his uniform on, the way his pressed suit hung off him; black, with white shirt and a matching black tie. Neil noted one or two of the locals checking him out and wondering whether they should hang around. The hoodie didn't even have to think about it and was out the door before you could say ''ello, 'ello, 'ello'. It seemed that some normals also had heightened senses when it came to things like that.

'Luke,' he said, nodding to the rep as he took his place at the pub table. Then he acknowledged Neil.

'Owen,' said Neil, raising his coke. 'Nice to see you again.'

'You too,' he said finally. 'I wish it were under better circumstances.'

Neil frowned, still looking to Luke for an explanation but getting nothing.

Owen caught the glance. 'I thought you might have heard...at least about Jack?'

Now Neil was really confused. 'What about him?'

'He's dead,' said Owen matter of factly, but his eyes betrayed the pain of those words.

Luke leaned forward on his chair and Neil almost spilled his drink. 'What? How?'

Owen looked down. 'Week before last, in a hotel room in Edinburgh. He was on tour with his band, one of the roadies found him. He'd OD-ed on drugs.' This wasn't too much of a shock, as Jack had always been fond of stronger vices than drink. If something was being passed around in a club, he'd usually be the one trying it. Also fitted with the kind of lifestyle he was used to these days: the gigs, the fans. Sex and drugs would be no stranger to Jack, not to mention the other…activities he was used to. But the fact he was dead? Jack was the strongest of them all, always had been. 'Thought there might have been more coverage of it by the media, but I guess they saw it as just another mid-list rocker paying the price for his own overindulgence.'

'I…I just can't believe it,' said Luke.

'Me either.' Neil was still in a state of shock, gripping his glass so tightly he was in danger of shattering it.

'There's more,' said Owen looking up again, eyebrows still stooping. He hadn't even asked for or bought a drink yet. They waited for him to continue, which he did eventually. 'Adrian…' He couldn't get the words out, but both Luke and Neil knew what was coming next wasn't good. 'Middle of last week, Adrian… Well, the police in his area are calling it a mugging that went sour – for Adrian *really* sour. He was stabbed.'

'Christ,' breathed out Luke. Neil knew how he felt: first Jack, now Adrian?

'Is he...?' Neil began.

Owen nodded. 'He was on his way back to his car after work. They got him in the car park, three times in the gut. His case and his wallet were missing when he was found.'

'Hold on!' said Neil, then lowered his voice. 'We're... I mean people like us, we're not that easy to...y'know...kill, are we?' Maybe he was hoping Owen had got it wrong somehow, that neither Jack nor Adrian were gone. They couldn't be, there was so much he wanted – *needed* – to say to them.

'We are not,' replied Owen. 'Which is why when I heard about them I did a little digging. I called in a few favours to get the reports on both Jack and Adrian, and do you know what I found?'

Luke and Neil shook their heads.

'Someone went to a lot of trouble to make these look like random events, but they weren't. It didn't make any difference to the investigation, so it was overlooked – but both Jack and Adrian's deaths were connected.'

'What are you talking about?' asked Luke.

'I'm talking about silver, Luke.' He let that particular bombshell sink in before continuing. 'It was found in Jack's system – trace particles of it that I think were probably in his drugs – and it was found in Adrian's stab wounds. Whoever it was killed him, they used a silver knife.'

Neil shook his head again, this time in disbelief. 'A coincidence, surely?' He had no idea how traces might have ended up in Jack's drugs, but a silver knife wasn't that uncommon, was it?

'Are you *fucking* listening to what I'm saying?' Owen was breathing hard through gritted teeth and his raised voice drew a few glances from the patrons of the Oak. 'Silver. Don't you see the link here?'

'You're not suggesting that the same people killed them both, are you?' Luke said.

'Not only that, I'm saying they knew Jack and Aide used to be part of the same pack. *Our* pack. That's why I got in touch with everyone who's left, to warn them.'

'But who…?' Luke was having as much trouble with all this as Neil, it seemed.

Owen swallowed before answering. 'In my line of work you see…you *hear* about a lot of crazy things. Nobody in authority makes connections like these, because nobody knows about people like us. But some folk do – out there. And some hunt them.'

Luke and Neil exchanged glances once more. 'Hunt?' said Luke, looking pained. It was interesting the way the dynamic had changed between Luke and Owen. Once upon a time, Luke might have been the one to call the shots – his job calling for confidence, for…balls. He had the looks as well, which meant the meat always flocked to him and he'd get first choice. But after years in the police force, Owen was the one with the confidence now; he was also apparently the one with insider information – however paranoid it might sound.

'This is crazy,' said Neil. 'Hunters…'

Owen leaned across the table. 'I'm telling you, they *exist*. And one or more are out there, trying to pick us off before the next full moon.' That was in a couple of days' time; Neil had been feeling the urges more and more frequently during its approach.

'You're off your head,' Neil told him. He'd been looking forward to tonight, albeit anxious about what the other guys might say to him.

But he'd just been told two of his oldest pals were dead, and another believed there was some kind of conspiracy to take down the rest. He wasn't going to sit around here listening to any more of it. Neil stood, making to leave. 'It's been nice catching up,' and he looked at Luke primarily when he said that, 'but I'll be going now, I reckon.'

Owen grabbed him by the wrist and this drew even more looks from customers. 'If I'm so crazy, where's Ryan? He's half an hour or more late.'

That wasn't anything unusual for Ryan, though. He'd always been known for his shit timekeeping, always the last to arrive at meetings. 'That doesn't mean anything,' Luke told Owen, echoing Neil's thoughts – and finding a little of the old courage that had once made him their unofficial leader.

Owen glared at him, nodded. 'You're right. Okay then, how about we all wait for him to show, see what *he* has to say about my theories.'

Luke looked at Neil. 'How about it? It has been a long time since we were all together like this.'

And would be again now, thought Neil –

his mind filling with memories of Jack and Aide, the former screaming out his lyrics at the mike, the latter with his cheeky chappie smirk. He just couldn't believe he would never see them again. Still, there was Luke here, there was Owen. He owed them something; owed them his time at least. 'Okay,' Neil said, sitting. 'But I can't be late back.'

Owen sneered at that. 'Still with the...' Neil could see him thinking about what to call her. '...little lady then?'

Neil said nothing; whatever he attempted in reply would be wrong, he knew that.

'I'll get you a drink,' said Luke to Owen. 'Still the usual? JD and Coke?'

'Make it a double,' said Owen. 'I've got a feeling I'm going to need it.'

They sat in silence until Luke returned, the buffer that would keep them from talking about her...

Julie.

...at least for the time being. The conversation was steered more towards what had happened to both Owen and Luke in the years since they'd seen each other. Luke was still repping, but growing increasingly tired of the lifestyle. In a strange sort of way, when he talked about it Neil got the distinct impression Luke was envious of him. Of what Neil had. Somewhere to call home, someone to return to at night.

(If he only knew.)

'It's just getting a bit old, you know?' he said, and now Neil saw the lines on his face marring those good looks. Time didn't stand still for anyone.

Past it...

Owen, as it turned out, was not just a policeman, but a plain clothes detective now. So the outfit he was wearing actually *was* his uniform. 'See, it's my job. I *detect*,' he told Neil. 'That's why you should be listening to me about Jack and Aide.'

Trying to avoid another argument, Luke said, 'A werewolf cop, eh? I think I saw a movie like that once.' Though his words were flippant, there was little humour to them. How could there be after what they'd been told that evening?

'And you Neil? Still working in the library?' asked Owen, with more than a hint of sarcasm in his voice.

'You bloody well know that's where I am, *detective.*' He'd mailed him there, for Christ's sake!

'Still stacking shelves and doling out romantic fiction to middle-aged women who can't get any?'

Neil ignored the remark. 'I'm senior librarian, if that's what you mean.'

Owen smirked. 'Senior, eh? I'm impressed. You get to shelve the really big books.'

Neil was beginning to wonder if the main reason Owen had got in touch was to have a go at him. 'Since when did you become such a dickhead? You used to be okay, Owen. Oh, right, I forgot – you joined the filth. We used to spend most of our time avoiding brushes with the law, remember that?'

Owen snorted. 'Better to be on the inside, then, isn't it. Now, I *am* the law.' It made him sound like fucking Judge Dredd or something, and it was all Neil could do to keep from bursting out laughing.

'Guys, guys...' said Luke, holding up his hands as if ready to keep them apart. He looked like a referee in a really bad boxing match.

Owen batted Luke's hand away. 'It's no more than you deserve, being stuck here like this…after—'

'After what? After meeting someone and settling down with them, after falling in love?'

Another snort. 'Love? Do me a favour. They're food, women like her. Always were, always will be.'

'Owen, people have to go their own way, live their own lives,' said Luke, which earned him a third snort.

'Bullshit. You reap what you sow.'

'What did you just say?' asked Neil.

'If you can sit there,' said the policeman, 'and tell me you're better off now than you were then, I'll—'

'I don't have to listen to this crap,' said Neil and this time when he got up nobody was going to stop him from leaving.

'Look at the time,' said Luke suddenly. It was almost half nine; they'd been waiting there an hour and a half. Ryan was late. *Really* late. Maybe literally. Neil paused, not needing anyone to stop him now.

'We should go to Ryan's place,' said Owen. 'See if he's okay.'

Luke nodded, his expression grim. 'I think you might be right.'

Owen rose now, and stood opposite Neil. 'You coming?'

Neil thought about it, but shook his head. It wasn't so much the promise he'd made Julie, it was more a case of not wanting to know for sure about Ryan. If they found him at home slashed to bits, then that really would mean there was a hunter – or *hunters* – running around after their hides (how much would a werewolf skin go for out there, anyway?...was there even a market?...probably, people would buy anything, and it would more than likely be a lot, even without the hair). No, they'd find Ryan safe and sound, probably drunk or asleep or—

'Doesn't have permission, y'see,' said Owen. 'That cow won't let him play past his bedtime.'

That was it; Neil lunged for Owen, growling. 'Just like you did with Ryan all those years ago, eh? Remember?' snapped Owen, grabbing hold of Neil's jumper in return.

Luke tried to force them apart, but the pair barged into him and he ended up knocking over the table they'd been sitting at. The landlord of the Oak, a burly man Neil knew called Kev – who was ironically hairier than any of them at present, with his lamb chop sideburns and shirt open to reveal the rings of black curls on his chest – was on them in seconds.

'Gentlemen,' he said, hauling them off each other. 'Fucking well pack it in!' He looked at Neil. 'I'm surprised at you. Never pegged you for the trouble-causing sort.'

'Oh, he's just full of surprises, aren't you?' Owen grunted. Then he pulled out his ID and the landlord shrank back. He must have been the only one in that place who hadn't realised Owen was Old Bill.

'I'm... I'm sorry,' said Kev, to Owen – but not to Neil.

Owen nodded. 'Don't worry about it. We were just going anyway.' He helped Luke to his feet. 'Come on.'

Owen strode off towards the door, but Luke lingered. He gave Neil one of his cards and asked for his number in return. Neil gave it, glancing over a few times to see Owen waiting impatiently by the door.

Then they were gone, leaving Neil with Kev. The landlord looked from the now empty doorway, to Neil, then said: 'Someone's going to have to pay for the damage, you know.'

Sighing, Neil took out his wallet.

*

By the time he arrived home, it was heading for eleven and Julie had gone to bed.

Eleven, on a Friday night? Neil cracked open another one of the tins of lager he'd bought from the off-license on his way back, slumping down in front of the TV, but kept the sound really low. He could hear still hear it, crystal clear.

He couldn't stop thinking about Jack, Adrian…Ryan. What Luke and Owen (the prick) might have found when they eventually got to his place. Who'd driven them there? Owen, after his JDs? Did that matter when he could just flash that ID of his? It would if he ended up wrapping them around a lamp-post or something, doing the hunters' job for them.

Neil shook his head. No, there *were* no hunters. No such thing…couldn't be.

But then there was Jack, Adrian and—

No, not Ryan. Of all of them, Neil owed him the biggest apology for what he'd done, what he'd said in the back of that van. It was no worse than what he'd been willing to do tonight when he went for Owen, he reminded himself. And the trigger both times:

Julie. Always Julie...

As if having some kind of radar, she appeared at the living room door. 'I *thought* I heard you.'

Bullshit, he'd barely made a noise – in spite of the drink. Neil knew how to be silent when he wanted to. She must have been listening out for him, like she was his fucking mother or something. What did she think he was going to do, come back with a woman on each arm? (A woman he'd then—)

'You've been drinking,' she said, pointing out the obvious. He was sitting there with a depleted six pack on his lap, knocking back the strong lager.

'So,' he said, looking at her properly now. She was wearing those hideous tartan pyjamas she was so fond of, and he loathed. A far cry from some of the stuff she'd worn for him years back to make him happy: the satin, the lace, the…not much at all. Those red and blue creations were designed to hide a woman's figure, but he could still see hers beneath it. Could still see how her breasts – maybe not as pert as they'd once been, but still full – pushed against the buttons of the top. Could see the way the material clung between her legs.

Neil looked away, his heartbeat up.

'So: you've been drinking *a lot*, by the looks of things. Had a good time with your mates, then I take it.'

Neil shrugged. *Not really*, he thought, *couple of them have died horrendously and another might well be slashed to ribbons, but apart from that…*

'That all you've got to say for yourself? Jesus, Neil—'

'Jesus what?' he said, rising.

'Jesus *Christ*, you're a loser. I don't know what I ever saw in you.'

Neil's pulse was quickening. He was staring at her, but wasn't fully seeing her. Whether it was the drink or what had happened back there in the pub, or just the closeness of that particular time of month, he didn't know but—

'Doesn't have permission, y'see. That cow won't let him play past his bedtime.'

'Love? Do me a favour. They're food, women like her. Always were, always will be.'

'They're meat…just meat.'

'Not getting past it, are you?'

'You don't know what you saw in me,' repeated Neil, his words slurring slightly. 'Here, let me remind you!'

He'd crossed the room in seconds, much quicker than anyone should have done, and it startled Julie. She stepped back. 'You…you keep away from me,' she told him.

'Or what?' said Neil, his words more *strange* than slurred now.

'You touch her. Any of you fucking so much as look at her…'

'Or…' she said, but all the usual self-assuredness was gone. 'Or I'll…' She was quivering, he could see it, hear the catch in her voice.

'I think…I think she's the one.'

'There aren't any "ones". Only the next meal.'

'You do know you can't have a normal life with this woman, don't you? How can you?'

He saw faces now, the faces of his friends –

as they were back then, as they probably had been when death found them. Jack, Adrian and—

'Why don't you do yourself a favour and leave her to us, we'll take care of the problem.'

Ryan's voice.

Maybe he should have listened.

'I-I'm going back to bed,' said Julie, turning from him. But it was too late, she'd woken something up other than herself and Neil wasn't sure whether he could get it to go to sleep again.

Wasn't sure he *wanted* to.

He grabbed her arm, but she shrugged it off. Julie made a break for the bedroom, then she was inside and trying to slam the door on him. Neil put his foot in the gap, pushed hard with all of his bodyweight on the door itself.

It gave, sending her reeling back. Her legs caught the edge of the bed and she fell onto it, the springs protesting, squeaking – just like they had once with his weight on top of her.

'Neil,' she moaned, crying, holding up her hand. 'Neil, please…you're scaring me.'

A grin broke its way free, and he pounced, covering the distance easily.

And now his weight was on her again, clawing at that stupid tartan, his mouth on her neck, feeling her pulse racing. As he tore his own clothes free, he recognised that look in her eye. He'd seen it once before when they'd first met, responding to his whims, his influence? No, something else; desiring the *animal* part of him. So she could feel as much of a creature as he was, abandon her humanity to him – to what they were doing. The beast with two backs.

'*This* is what you saw in me,' he said, shredding her pyjama bottoms and entering her, ramming into her so hard her breath was taken from her. Then her hands were at the base of his neck, urging him on. Faster, faster. Harder...

Until neither of them could fight it any more.

*

He was vaguely aware of a phone going off, a trill ring-tone that told him it wasn't the house phone, but his old mobile – somewhere on the bedroom floor, after falling out of his trouser pocket last night.

Neil rubbed his face, rising and glancing across at the naked body lying next to him. There were claw marks down Julie's back, not that deep but still raw. At first he thought the body might be a corpse, but then he saw the steady rise and fall of her shoulders with each breath.

Things were a bit of a blur, just flashes, snatches of what they – what *he'd* – done. But he did remember that in the heat of it all, his wife had responded, as if on some primal level. Just like before, just like when they'd first met. Was it as simple as that, a vicious circle? As they'd lost that part of their relationship, as he'd sacrificed everything just to be with her, she'd started to lose interest in him that way?

The phone continued to ring, and he chased away the thoughts, swinging over the side of the bed to snatch it up. As he did so he couldn't help smirking when he saw Julie's tartan pyjamas, not far away, completely ruined.

He checked the time on the phone before accepting the call; it was 1:15 in the afternoon. They'd slept the morning away, which was hardly surprising seeing as they'd been up most of the night. A good thing neither of them was working today. There was no caller ID, but he did recognise the number vaguely as the one Luke had given him back at the pub. He pressed the green button.

'Hello,' he said, suddenly lowering his voice on the second syllable so as not to disturb Julie.

'Neil, thank Christ!' It was definitely Luke's voice, but even more panicked than it had been when they'd gone their separate ways.

'Is everything all right?' asked Neil, realising that it was probably the most stupid thing he'd ever said. Of course it wasn't all right; he could tell that from Luke's tone, even if he didn't know why the man was ringing.

'No it bloody isn't. It's Ryan.'

Neil pinched the skin between his eyes, head sagging. 'You found him, then?'

'Yes, we found him.' This was the bit where they described how messed up he'd been when they broke into his house and— 'He's been in an accident. At least that's what they're saying.'

'What?'

'He's still alive, *barely*. It was a hit and run driver, a few days ago. When we got no answer from his place and figured out there was nobody home, Owen did some checking around. He's actually pretty good at all this detective stuff. Ryan's in The General hospital, banged up pretty bad.'

'I'm really sorry to hear that,' said Neil, though wasn't there another part of him which was relieved? That Ryan hadn't actually been murdered; that he was still alive. A hit and run was better than being murdered, surely...*if* that's what actually happened to Aide and Jack.

'You need to get down here,' said Luke.

Neil looked over his shoulder at Julie, stirring. 'Look, it's a bit difficult right now.'

'Give me that,' Neil heard another voice say, then suddenly it was Owen talking to him. 'Neil, get your fucking arse down to the hospital – *right now!* We've got things to talk about.'

'I...' He wasn't about to do that just because Owen was ordering him to. At the same time, he did want to see Ryan – and his old mate was hurt, not dead.

'Neil, fucking well get—'

He felt a hand on his back and he snapped off the phone, whirling to see Julie sitting up.

'Neil?' she said, softly – the bolshiness from when he'd got back last night gone. 'Who was that?'

'A friend,' he told her honestly.

'One of the ones you saw yesterday?'

He nodded. She dipped her green eyes momentarily, not sure whether to believe him or not. 'Neil…look, I think we need to talk.'

'We've got things to talk about.'

'I can't right now. I've got to go, something's come up.'

Julie frowned. 'Something's come up?' she repeated, the hard edge returning. '*This* is something too, isn't it?'

'My friend's in the hospital.'

'What, the one who's ringing?'

'No, another one.' He realised how ridiculous it sounded, like an excuse to get out of talking to Julie. Maybe it was. He didn't really want to sit here and chat about what had happened, his head was too full of other crap.

'I see,' she said, drawing her knees up and folding her arms around them.

Neil went to the wardrobe, pulling out fresh clothes – that weren't torn – and began to dress. 'We'll talk when I get back. I promise.'

She just stared at him blankly, watching as he grabbed his wallet and keys and left the bedroom. Neil shut the door behind him, leaning back on it and hanging his head.

Then he left the house without looking back.

*

When Neil arrived at the hospital, he hadn't been expecting Ryan to look like this.

The guy might as well have been cut to pieces, because he was hardly recognisable. 'Hit and Run' Luke had said, but Ryan looked like he'd been hit repeatedly, then backed over several times – in fact he looked like the car had been dropped on him from a great height.

Neil also knew that he'd recover. In fact, he should have been getting better already, so Neil was puzzled when Luke told him that their friend's condition was worsening if anything.

'Owen,' said Luke, nodding to the policeman sat outside in the corridor (only two being allowed to sit with Ryan at any given time), 'he thinks there might have been some silver involved again. You know, maybe on the bumper or something? Hard to ask without tipping off the staff.'

'Again with the silver?' This was getting ridiculous. Now not only was Owen saying that Jack's overdose and Adrian's mugging was by a fictional hunter or group of them, now they'd also run over Ryan? 'Are you buying this shit?' Neil asked Luke.

He shrugged. 'Kinda makes sense.'

And would explain why he wasn't getting *any* better.

Neil looked back again at Owen. Despite having 'commanded' Neil come, he'd pulled a face when he'd actually arrived. 'She finally let you off the leash, then?' Owen had said.

'Fuck off,' Neil replied. He hadn't come here for Owen, and definitely hadn't come to discuss his private life; he'd come to see Ryan.

Now Neil approached the bed, eyes like slits as he took in more of the injuries – Ryan's face so swelled it looked like it was about to pop. 'I'm sorry, man,' he whispered; for the state he was in, but also for what he'd done back in Jack's van. He thought once more that they'd spent the last several years so close by, but might as well have been on different continents. If only he'd picked up a phone or something. 'So, what are his chances?' asked Neil finally.

Another shrug from Luke. 'Owen's been waiting to talk to a doctor – not even flashing that badge of his has got him anywhere so far. He's off his patch, for one thing.'

Neil was just about to say something else, when he spotted Owen rising. The policeman called to them from the door and they rushed over to an increasingly distracted Owen.

'There!' he shouted, pointing. They both looked, but saw nothing. 'A bloke, he was standing watching from the end of that corridor,' Owen told them.

'What the hell are you on about?' said Neil.

'When I looked up, he looked away – but I *saw* him.'

'Probably just another visitor,' Luke offered.

'I'm telling you, there was something dodgy about him.'

'Owen, you can't—' began Neil, but Owen was off, up the corridor and sprinting past doctors and nurses.

Sighing, Luke ran after him – and Neil ran

after them both, intending to give the copper another piece of his mind when he caught up. Him and his overactive imagination – that was the only dodgy thing around here. A wild goose chase, that's all this whole bloody thing was.

By the time they'd turned a couple of corners, Owen had vanished. Luke sniffed the air, but there were too many other scents here to pick him out. Too many people: patients, staff and visitors alike. 'Maybe he got in the lift?' Neil suggested. It was entirely possible, but how would they know which floor he went to? After searching a couple of floors up in the maze-like building, Neil made another suggestion – for Luke to call Owen. But he couldn't do that inside the hospital itself.

When they got to the main entrance, Luke already had the number on speed-dial. He shook his head. 'Can't reach him.'

There was a group of people gathering outside, and figures in scrubs were pushing past Luke and Neil, obviously in a hurry to check out the next emergency case coming in.

Then they saw who it was.

Neil pulled a couple of bystanders aside to

get a better view; Luke followed in his wake. And there, on the concrete in front of them – the medics working furiously on him – was Owen. His limbs were sticking out at odd angles, like some kind of weird insect tipped over on its back. And the base of his skull was leaking – obviously cracked or even smashed, it was letting out blood and quite possibly other vital fluids meant to be contained.

'What happened?' Neil heard someone ask.

'Dunno, I think he threw himself off the roof,' came the reply.

No. Not Owen. That's what this might *look* like: a random suicide. But it wasn't. He'd been thrown off the roof and both Neil and Luke knew it.

'He's crashing. We're losing him,' said one of the women in scrubs kneeling in Owen's pooling blood. And it was only now, as she opened up the man's shirt, that they saw it. The chain around his neck. Easily mistaken for a necklace or charm, they didn't have to touch it to know what the thing was made from. A metal that Owen would never have worn in a million years, but would have ensured his fall from the building was fatal.

The woman pounded on his chest, trying to get his heart beating again, but it was a futile effort. Even if Neil or Luke had risked barging in, taking the chain off – without being branded thieves – the damage had already been done.

Open-mouthed, they looked from Owen's prone body to each other. Then they both swore at the same time.

Where Owen had gone nobody would be reaching him again, on a phone or otherwise.

*

There didn't seem much doubt anymore.

Owen had gone after the hunter (or hunters, they still hadn't established how many of them there were) and got himself killed. The old gang *were* being picked off, and the one member who knew the most – who had the skills that might help them get out of this mess – was now gone.

Luke and Neil searched the hospital again, but without knowing who they were looking for, it seemed pretty pointless. Owen was the only one who'd got a look at the guy that had done this (one of a team?). Besides which, what more chance would they stand than Owen?

Ironically, by bringing them together like this, Owen had actually made the task of killing them even easier. 'Do you think that's what they had in mind?' asked Luke. 'Maybe they counted on the fact Owen would put all the pieces together and get in touch with us.'

'Maybe,' said Neil. 'Now there's only us left to deal with.'

'Ryan,' Luke reminded him.

'He's dying,' Neil sighed. 'We both know it's only a matter of time. Whoever's doing this is nothing if not thorough. They'd *make sure* he wasn't going to wake up again.'

They had two choices now, get the hell out of town and hope they weren't being tracked (it was a slim chance) or try and stay alive till tomorrow and deal with the hunter(s) in their altered forms.

Neither option was very appealing.

'Well, I don't know about you,' said Luke, 'but I'm bailing.' It was something the younger Luke would never have said, would never have *done*, and Neil thought again how much he'd changed. Owen might have been a pain in the arse these days, but right now Neil would have swapped Luke for the arrogant detective any day of the week; at least Owen would have put up a fight. 'If you've got any brains, you'll do the same.'

But it wasn't as simple as that, was it? Luke had no ties, but Neil had:

Julie. Always Julie.

'Shit,' said Neil, dialling the number for home as Luke waved goodbye – off back to the hotel to pack his stuff, then drive into the sunset. The phone was picked up on the third ring. 'Julie... Julie, listen to me—'

'Neil? Where are you? You've been gone hours.'

'That's not important. I need you to—'

'Not important? *Not important?*' she was practically screaming the last bit. 'You do what you did last night, then leave after getting a phone call today telling me some stupid story about a hospital...'

'It wasn't a story, look—'

'I've had it with this bullshit. I'm going away for a bit, Neil.'

'Good, that's good.' He regretted the words as soon as they were out of his mouth. He meant it was good because it was dangerous to be around him right now, but he couldn't explain that to *her*.

'Good? You think it's *good* I'm leaving you?' Now not even dogs...or people like Neil...could hear her, she was so shrill. And without being there, he had no way of talking to her (*influencing* her?), calming her down. 'Fuck you, Neil.' She hung up the phone with a click.

He tried ringing her back, but she'd left it off the hook – and her mobile was turned off. 'Shit!' he repeated. In spite of how dangerous it was, he had to go back now. Neil crossed the road to flag down a taxi when his phone rang. He answered it quickly, not even looking at the ID.

'Julie?'

'Neil... Neil, you have to come, right now!' It was Luke, and he sounded terrified.

'Where are you?'

'At the hotel. There's someone. Neil you have to—' The connection fizzled out, and Neil had no more luck getting back in touch with Luke than he had done with Julie.

When the taxi pulled up and he got inside,

the driver asked: 'Where to, mate?'

Neil thought for a moment, then said: 'Wanderer's Lodge, Hadley Street'.

*

Though Luke hadn't mentioned the room number he was staying in, and Neil knew that reception would never tell him, he was easily able to track his friend's scent. The corridors were relatively free of people, and those who were staying there had locked themselves away in their rooms, watching TV, screwing, or getting ready to head off for a Saturday night out. Again, that would have been Neil so long ago; not in a hotel room – but preparing to hit the clubs, on the prowl with his mates (who were all but dead now, and in the space of the last month). Plus which, with every hour that passed, Neil's senses were growing keener. By tomorrow night, they'd be at their sharpest.

Room 320, on the third floor. That's where Luke's scent led him. He was about to knock on the door, when he saw it was already open a crack. Neil contemplated running away, but after what he'd thought of Luke for doing the same, it seemed more than a little hypocritical. He toed open the door, then scanned the small room. There was nobody inside, but he could still smell Luke's scent. That stopped once he made it into the room itself.

The light was on in the bathroom, so Neil followed it – still poised to tackle anyone who might leap out at him. He could smell the coppery aroma of blood, but diluted somehow. Making his way inside, he saw the tub there filled with red water. Luke was in that water, stripped to his boxers, staring up at Neil with glassy eyes. His veins had been opened, the razor used still on the side of the bath. Neil didn't need to examine it to know that this, too, was made from silver. Once more, whoever had done this had covered themselves – another 'suicide'. There was no way anyone, apart from him, would think otherwise.

Shaking his head, Neil backed out of the room – knowing that the sight of Luke like this would follow him to the grave. How long he'd have until he faced that scenario was another matter.

He exited the room, left the hotel – looking over his shoulder the whole time. Luke had had the right idea: get out, run before the hunters could kill them. Only he'd been too late, the pursuers too clever.

Just as their enemy was being clever right now: a car waiting, crawling down the street – lights coming on when the driver saw Neil, dazzling him. His only warning was the revving of a powerful engine, and then it was after him. Neil ran, very aware now of his belly and how much faster he would have been if he'd kept in Luke's shape (though it hadn't really helped Luke much, had it?). He needed to get to a more densely populated area, the nightlife area for example. But the driver of the car had other ideas, blocking off the way Neil was going to go and more or less forcing him down a side street.

Was this how Ryan had felt when he was mown down? Neil wondered. Had he even had this much time before the car rammed into him? A car, Neil saw as he looked back, that did indeed have a silver bumper – with rough edges that, if they caught him, would definitely tear into his legs. Neil skidded round another corner, praying to see some signs of life – someone, anyone out on the streets. But they were all gravitating to the more exciting parts of town right now, which left the way clear for the hunters to run Neil to ground. The car was gaining on him again, but Neil did at least have one advantage. It had been a long time since he'd been out this far, but the town hadn't changed that much, and there had been a time of day when he'd known these streets blindfolded. Better than whoever was chasing him, certainly, because there was a shortcut this way to the old canal.

Neil ran down one deserted street and up another, the car still behind but having to go slowly in unfamiliar territory.

Nearly there, nearly there, he was telling himself, puffing out breath as he went. What he would do when he actually got there, Neil hadn't really figured out – he just knew that cars couldn't drive on water, so that's where he should be heading. The car sped up when that water came into view, obviously realising what Neil had in mind.

Neil was running towards the railing which stopped people from falling into the canal, maybe thinking he could leap that, climb down the side. But he didn't get a chance; the car pulled up alongside and clipped Neil. He was pitched over the railings, and suddenly was falling. It seemed to take a long time to finally hit the water, and when he did, it felt like it was hitting him back. He might have banged his head on something, but Neil definitely blacked out, letting both the darkness and the water take him.

*

When he woke, he ached all over.

He'd been pitched up on the bank some way down the canal, and it was light again. Neil blinked, coughed, and experimentally raised his head. That had been a bad idea. He looked at his watch, but it had stopped when he fell – was forced – into the dirty water.

It still said 8:30 pm

Had to be the next day, though. Sunday. *Damn*, he was lucky to be alive. His head was sore, and when he touched the crown there was a lump where he must have knocked it on something before sinking.

Probably looked like he was a goner. Probably also why the person or people after him didn't come down to check, to finish the job properly. Neil lifted himself up, letting out a cry at the pain he was in. Luckily, that bumper hadn't caught him or this would have been so much worse. He'd be okay in a couple of hours, three or four at most – and later on was a full moon, which would see him growing stronger and stronger...

He was soaking, and he was hungry.

It probably wasn't the best of ideas, but Neil decided to head home.

*

He'd drawn some strange looks on the bus he'd caught, not least because of the smell, but Neil ignored them. It was late afternoon a church clock informed him, not long till evening. He'd made sure he wasn't being followed – as best he could, anyway – and had watched his own house for about half an hour before entering, just to make sure it wasn't being staked out.

It wasn't, he concluded, but entered through the back door anyway. At least Julie was away from all this – had left hating him, but was safe.

Or so he'd thought.

The hunter(s) had been thorough as always, making it appear as if a burglar had broken in through the side window, that Julie had surprised the criminal and paid the price for it. Why hadn't she gone like she said she was going to? If only she'd...

Neil went to the body, face down on the living room rug amongst the books and DVDs thrown there to make it look like the place had been ransacked. He turned her over, but knew Julie was dead. Her neck had been snapped. Tears were welling in Neil's eyes, and as he sniffed them up, he smelt something else.

His wife hadn't been the only one to die that day. It probably wouldn't have been detectable if he hadn't been who he was, probably wouldn't even have shown up on a test yet – but Neil knew. Not only that, he *smelt* what his son might have become had his life not been snuffed out before it really began: sensed all the triumphs and the losses he would have gone through; saw the magic tricks he would have learned from his father as a kid, a hobby that would have stayed with him for life; shared in the knowledge he would have learnt at school, then university; saw the job he would do – following his mother into teaching; saw the faces of all the girls he might have dated, before finally marrying one of them; saw the grandchildren Neil would now never have…

All lost, all gone.

He wouldn't have carried Neil's burden, either – having inherited more genes from Julie than him. His son would have led a normal life, free from being hunted like his father had been this weekend.

Neil bared his teeth and then he growled. Then he began to howl…

He sniffed again. This time he smelt the interloper.

And now he had a trail to follow.

*

It ended in an alleyway, behind a row of nightclubs, the trail and that very long weekend.

The place was familiar to Neil, one of his old stomping grounds. It made him wonder whether he'd been lured here, whether following the scent was just another trap. If it was, he didn't care anymore. Didn't care about much at all as he crouched on a fire escape, stripped, observing the man standing with his back to Neil in the shadows cast by the full moon above.

The car – the one used to try and run Neil down – was at the head of the alley, abandoned, and the man who presumably owned it was just waiting out in the open. He looked to be alone, but might simply be the bait (others could have masked their scent somehow – they were sneaky bastards, he'd seen that). Neil might not care, but that didn't mean he was insane. And he wanted his revenge.

Now the man was crouching, too, just like Neil. He bent, the echo of his cracking knees reverberating throughout the alley, but was almost swallowed by the thumping techno beat from some of the clubs round the front.

What the hell was he doing? Neil squinted, looked around again for any sign of companions. Nothing…

The man was rising again, preparing to walk back to his car. If Neil was going to strike, it had to be now.

'Fuck it,' he whispered, then leapt down from the fire escape – transforming as he did so. (Getting back into shape; he'd show them who was past it!) He hadn't done this at will for a long time, and the quickness of it took him by surprise. His whole body tingled as the new hairs appeared, his eyes taking on that yellow and scarlet cast that gave them almost infra-red capabilities, tongue growing as his teeth lengthened and became much more pointed.

He landed awkwardly, not with the grace and skill he'd once been able to boast, and it alerted the man ahead of him – who opened his mouth in surprise. If he was shocked, then it was the first time since all this began they – all right, Neil, because he was the only one left – had the upper hand. That didn't last long.

The man pulled something from his jacket and aimed it at Neil. There was no bang, as he might have expected, but Neil felt the impact of a projectile in his shoulder – hard and sharp. A bolt from a handheld crossbow. A *silver* bolt that stung like someone had just rammed a red-hot poker into him.

Neil howled again, this time in pain – but

he had the presence of mind to dodge the next two bolts fired, one flying over his head, the other whizzing past his thigh.

Clawing at the wound with nails that had matched his teeth in growth, Neil managed to rip out the bolt and toss it aside. The wound still burned, but wouldn't prove fatal.

Neil lunged forwards, using his powerful legs to propel himself. The man was trying to reload his crossbow, but couldn't do it in time and so abandoned that idea in favour of retreating to his car.

Neil came bounding up behind, but if he thought it was going to be that easy, he was sadly mistaken. The man turned, suddenly, and lashed out with a chain – slightly thicker than the one he must have used on Owen, this nevertheless had the same effect. It wound itself around Neil's neck, half-choking him when the man tugged hard. That same burning sensation struck Neil, and if the hunter had a weapon to hand he might have been able to finish the werewolf off while he was in his weakened condition.

But Neil gathered up enough strength to lash out with a claw, which only missed the hunter by millimetres. Closer now to the man, Neil was able to take in more of his features. He was older than Neil had expected. Older even than he was... The man's silver-grey hair was still hanging on to the remnants of a darker colour, but the lines criss-crossing his face gave him away completely. Though he'd obviously looked after himself better than Neil, this man had to be pushing sixty.

The hunter let go of the chain and stumbled backwards, breaking into a dash for the car. Neil dropped to his knees, tearing at the chain around his neck.

She finally let you off the leash, then?

Owen's harsh words made him think of Julie, and then he thought of her lying on the living room floor, thought about both her and the baby dying at this man's hands.

And that just made Neil go wild.

He shrugged off the chain and rose, roaring, into the night air. The thumping of the music from the clubs kept pace with the rhythm of his heart, accompanied the pumping of the blood around the hunter's body, which Neil could hear. He bounded after him, faster and faster.

The hunter had made it to the vehicle, though, and was sliding inside, sliding the key into the ignition at the same time. He gunned the engine and began reversing at Neil.

The wolf hadn't been expecting that move, and when the car connected with him, it knocked him back into the alleyway. Luckily, the rear bumper wasn't silver – there was no fire when the car hit Neil – so he rose, quickly, shaking his head and snarling. The hunter had braked after hitting the wolf, but now floored the accelerator again, clouds of smoke pluming from the tyres. He was planning to finish off the job, but Neil had other ideas.

He climbed onto the boot, claws digging into the metal so he could haul himself up. Then he was on the roof, ripping through it like paper, to get to the man inside – who braked once more, attempting to throw Neil off. It only succeeded in swinging the wolf around, so that his legs hung over the front of the car and one knee cracked the windscreen.

Snarling, Neil continued to pull away pieces of the roof, like a child tearing wrapping off a Christmas present. The man was trying to open his driver's side door, but it was jammed, forcing him to go for the passenger one instead.

He just about got out as Neil forced his way in, the man crawling away back into the alley. Neil clambered out again through the roof just as the car hit a wall and came to a stop. He waited for the hunter to get to his feet. The man half-turned as Neil leaped on him, pinning him to the ground. He let out a cry but refused to show any fear.

'Go on!' he screamed into Neil's face. 'Do it, you monster!' It wasn't the wisest thing to say when you had a werewolf towering over you. 'Do it so I can be with Tammy again.'

Neil was about to sink his teeth in when he paused.

Tammy? What was he talking about? He sniffed at the man, sucking up who he was, why he was here. Neil looked around, seeing the flowers the man had left on the ground not far away, and everything slotted into place.

That night, that last night he'd been out with the lads – the girls, the brunette, the tanned one, and:

Tammy.

Tammy with her blonde hair, arms outstretched so Adrian and Owen could feast on her, then the rest could later. Tammy, who had lied about her age to get into those clubs in the first place. Tammy, who was only fifteen, but had looked much older. And they'd taken her life away – she'd only led half of one anyway. Tammy, the (strawberry) blonde girl who'd had Julie's face in that alley.

Now Neil saw this man in front of him, *really* saw him. Her father, being given the news that she'd disappeared. He was the only parent she'd had, after her mother had died of cancer when Tammy was just five. So he'd searched for her, all over the place – quitting his job and living on savings, picking up tracking skills as he went. They'd *created* this hunter (you reap what you sow, right? reap what you…), and he'd finally stumbled on the truth years later – an ageing rocker who couldn't keep his mouth shut, telling stories about wolves and killings to impress his druggie friends. They hadn't believed a word, but – on hearing those rumours – the hunter had. He'd put two and two together, gone back and worked out that Jack had been around the same time Tammy—

A bit more digging, and he had a few more

names. He had Owen's, a policeman (so no point going to them). But what he could do was use the man to get the whole pack before the next full moon. Get them, and anyone else mixed up with them. Anyone like:

Julie.

A single tear ran from the wolf's eye, and the father frowned. Neil morphed back into human form, his shoulder still a mess, neck still red-raw. 'There was no need for any of... I ended all this a long time ago.'

The man said nothing.

'I'm sorry,' said Neil, letting the hunter drop and getting up. 'But I didn't do it. It wasn't me who killed your daughter.' Though God knows, he'd killed enough of other people's. Now this man had taken Neil's friends from him (if he could still call them that), had taken Julie too, and his son – who hadn't even been given half a chance at life.

But they'd taken his Tammy first, they'd taken the one thing that really mattered in his life. In spite of everything, could Neil really kill this man?

'Go on, get out of here,' he snapped.

As with most things in his life, though, the

decision was taken out of Neil's hands. Neil was ready to just let him go – regardless of the fact he might still come after him once this time of the month was over. Regardless of the hunger for blood this hunter had stirred up inside *him*.

But the father got up and rushed Neil – drawing a hidden blade that had probably done for Adrian when he was 'mugged'. Neil acted instinctively as it arced down towards his back, twirling and transforming at the same time (it didn't take him by surprise this time; he *enjoyed* it).

Neil sliced through the man's wrist and both the hand and knife fell to the ground. Then he was on the older man, biting, clawing, sucking and eating. It was the first decent, fresh meal he'd had in years, and it invigorated him. Neil knew the wolf could leave no part of this man alive, couldn't pass this on to him because it was…well, it was a gift really (*not* an affliction, *not* a curse).

As Neil finished up on the father, he reflected on how he really should be thanking the man. Not just for filling his belly, but also for reminding him what he was at heart, freeing him – freeing him from Julie? – and giving him a fresh start. There was no need for him to feel old anymore, or past it, not if he didn't want to. He'd only been living half a life himself, but he wasn't even halfway *through* his life – and there was so much time to catch up on.

When he was done, Neil shape-shifted again and went back to the car, climbing in. The engine was still running. As battered as it was, the vehicle would make it to the outskirts of the city, where he'd dump it and then steal another. It was time to move on, to get out of here. To live the life Luke had been living, or Jack.

As Neil sat behind the wheel, gunning that engine, he stared at the entrance of the alleyway.

And, for the first time in a long while, he thought about the future.

Lifetime

He couldn't exactly say it felt good to be back, but it felt right.

The town, his old town – his hometown...once upon a time. Not that he'd been born here, or even grew up here. No, this was the place he'd chosen to make a life for himself. Where he'd *lived* – back when he was young. A lifetime ago now.

Neil sat in the car, not the same one he'd fled in all those years ago – twenty-five years ago to be precise – as that had been stolen, and this was a hirer, but it was an eerily similar make. And here he was again, back where it had all begun...in more ways than one. He'd already done the tour, because Neil had landed again on these shores a few days ago now, ferry hopping across the channel for the final leg of his journey. As he'd driven down the motorway, one of Brutal's best albums blaring away, he'd wondered what he would find when he got here, how it might have changed in the time he'd been away – *stayed* away.

Nothing could have prepared him for quite how bad things had become, though – the shocking state of the economy having done its worst. In fact, it was almost like driving through a ghost town to begin with, hardly anyone on the streets, and those he did spot looked like pale imitations of people – either that or they looked haunted themselves. Storefronts were boarded over or had faded 'going out of business' banners hanging in darkened windows. What few shops remained had to be struggling, Neil reasoned. The library where he'd slaved away for all those years, working his way up to become senior librarian in fact before taking off without even letting them know, had also been shut down. That was hardly a surprise, however, given how many cuts had been made in government funding, and how the 'net had made libraries, vaster than his old one could ever hope to be, available to people at the click of a mouse.

Neil had found himself breaking in for a

final look around – especially down at the basement where he used to lock himself away at that special time of the month. He hadn't lingered too long; it was upsetting for him to see the state of the bookcases, the abandoned tomes covered in cobwebs. Forgotten about, unloved, unwanted. Ancient and all alone.

He could relate.

In fact, the town in general seemed to reflect how he felt at the moment. Lost, world-weary and old...very, very old. It occurred to him that they'd always been connected, that no matter where he'd wandered it had always been calling to him. Nagging at him to return until he could no longer ignore it, until he felt compelled to return regardless of how he'd left things. They'd aged together, it seemed – and in spite of the fact he didn't have as many aches and pains as the average man of seventy (his kind were more resilient than normal humans) he still felt the weight of his years. When he looked in the mirror, it was a white-haired guy with too many lines creasing his face that was staring back at him. But at least he *had* hair, Neil often reminded himself. He'd always have hair – *too much* of it at a certain point in the month, as it happened. And while he no longer had the beer belly he'd developed during his time playing at having a normal existence, his body wasn't in as good a shape as it had been even a decade ago – no matter how many push-ups he attempted in the mornings, no matter how much he jogged or star-jumped.

It was a far cry from the fresh-faced student who'd attended uni here, met his old friends, his pack, here – who'd been just as young, just as naïve. Hadn't worked out just how rotten the world could be yet, how unfair, how unjust. How there were always consequences to your actions – or, as his mate Owen (his *dead* mate Owen) might have said: 'You reap what you sow.'

It took him a while to build himself up to the house, mind: the house he'd lived in for a major part of his life here, after getting married and 'settling down' for a while. After meeting Julie, the catalyst for splitting up his merry little band. The signal for starting to grow up, he'd thought; becoming tamed and boring his friends had probably figured. There was someone else living there when he finally plucked up enough courage to drive by, other cars in the driveway. Which felt weird, as did imagining those other people inside, sitting watching TV in the lounge, making love in the bedroom where—

Neil had shaken his head, tears in his eyes. Wasn't it bad enough that he had nightmares about it, seeing Julie pull her legs up to her chest in bed, hugging her knees the last time... Then lifeless on the floor, neck snapped, yet hearing her voice as he had on the phone, those final words she'd spoken to him:

'Fuck you, Neil!'

She'd just told him she was leaving, and he'd said to her, 'Good'. Good, for Christ's sake! But all he'd meant was it would be better for her to be away, out of town and out of danger. Not that he *wanted* her to go. Not after the night they'd just shared, one that topped any of the other nights they'd slept together – even back when they first met. How was he to know that it was already too late, that the maniac who'd targeted Neil and his friends already had Julie in his sights?

Neil had seen the toys then, in the garden. These people had kids – *a* kid at any rate. A kid like the one they'd created, conceived that night; a son whose life had been stolen even before it had really begun. And, worse still, it was Neil's fault it had happened.

He'd had to drive off then before he lost it completely. Neil wondered if they knew what had happened in that place so long ago? It was doubtful, hardly a selling point – unless you were one of those sickos who got off on murder houses. For a fraction of a second he thought about going back and telling them:

'Don't you understand, my wife and son were murdered here! In this fucking house where you're living your life, completely oblivious and happy!'

It would be unfair to do that to them, but then again that was life, wasn't it? He thought of the consequences thing again and decided against it – wasn't their fault, what had happened there. Why should they have to pay for it? Reap what he and his pals had sown?

'Fuck you...'

Julie's words again, drifting through his mind while he was awake now – and Neil certainly had been fucked, hadn't he? They all had. Jack and Adrian even before they'd come back together again, one poisoned the other stabbed. Owen, who'd become a detective since Neil last saw him, and figured out what was happening – that they were being hunted and picked off – had been thrown from the roof of the hospital Ryan had also found himself in after being run over.

Dead. All dead.

And wasn't Neil staying in the very hotel where his last friend, Luke, had met his end? Staged as a suicide, submerged in crimson bath water with a razorblade by the side of him; a *silver* blade, to be precise – had to be. Just as silver was used in all the other killings to some extent, the only way to be sure people like Neil *were* actually dead.

He'd been surprised to find the hotel on Hadley Street was still open for business – though it had been absorbed by a familiar chain and was no longer called The Wanderer's Lodge. Probably not as surprised as the woman at the desk, however, when he'd asked for a room: 'Any room apart from 320.' She'd frowned at him and simply nodded, perhaps assuming he had a thing about those numbers or that he'd had a bad sexual experience in there? He didn't give a shit, he just needed a place to stay and this was the only real option in town… Neil just didn't want to lay his head down in a room where Luke had bought it, even if he wasn't planning on staying for too long.

It had all been a preamble, a prelude to tonight. To this pilgrimage he was undertaking. He'd begun by driving to the park just off Milton Street where he used to meet up with his buddies before a night out when he was in his twenties. Leaving the car by the side of the road, he'd entered the empty park and sat down on a bench by the lake to watch the ducks and geese, to look at the trees – the leaves still green for the moment, though they wouldn't be for long now they were entering the autumn season. It had been quiet, pleasant, and his mind had conjured up more ghosts from the past. Luke leaning over and looking at his reflection in the lake – combing his hair back, making sure those model looks were up to scratch for pulling later on; Jack, fresh from practising with his band – who'd have ever thought they'd make it big? – pushing Luke's shoulder so he overbalanced, but making sure the lad didn't fall in. Ryan and Adrian mucking about, playing 'keepy-uppy' with empty cans of beer they'd drained, and talking about the match... Calling Neil over to join in, which of course he'd been happy to do, while Luke and Jack shared a stubby cigarette.

Those visions faded soon enough, and before he was ready – but Neil knew it was time to head off anyway, to take in the next leg of the journey. Time for a quick pint at The Oak, which did still have its original name and was still being run by Kev, though he probably should have retired long ago. Once burly, he'd lost weight since last Neil had seen him; looked ill in fact. Neil gave a sniff as the man served him and, yes, detected the unmistakable whiff of cancer. The man only had a year left, tops; shouldn't even be working, let alone on his own – although there weren't more than a couple of people in the whole pub. Nevertheless, he remembered Neil.

'Bitter, right?' Kev had said.

Neil didn't want to correct him, his taste for that particular drink having vanished around the same time he had – replaced by various drinks depending on where he was in the world at the time. But, when in Rome. He'd nodded at the man.

Kev winked. 'I never forget a customer, *or* what they drink. Been a while, though.'

'It has,' Neil admitted.

'Where've you been hiding, then?'

The landlord's choice of words made Neil flinch, so accurate without him even knowing it. That was exactly what Neil had been doing, hiding away. He'd told himself that he'd fled the area not just because of the devastation he was leaving behind – and the awkward questions that would inevitably follow – but because it was time to get back to the old ways again, to return to the old Neil who'd embraced his baser instincts. Told himself that and lived like it for a long time, until it got boring. Just wasn't the same as when the boys had been with him, plus he couldn't ignore the fact that he *was* getting older by the day. His heart simply wasn't in it any more: the chase. It just wasn't any…fun. Some of that had to do with what had happened because of their antics, most of it was just because he wasn't the same person he had been back then. Events had changed him irrevocably.

Every one of his victims, all the women he'd 'pushed' – necessarily older women now, because his days of hanging around in clubs were long since gone – all the ladies he'd persuaded to come with him, he'd had to force himself to devour. He'd met a lot of them at singles nights, which attracted a certain kind of desperate older person, so in fairness Neil hadn't really needed to nudge them that hard (and he'd seen she-wolves too, doing the same thing with *their* prey at a few of those events – but he'd kept out of their way…mostly…because he knew for a fact that the females could be just as vicious, if not more so, than the males he'd encountered). Many had been willing to go with Neil anyway, thought he seemed like a nice guy. And with each sniff, he'd gained a greater sense of who they were and how they'd ended up alone: divorces; affairs; shyness in their youth. Often he even convinced himself that he'd be doing them a favour by killing them.

But he'd also been cursed with seeing their possible futures, what 'might be' for them. Some had kids, and would have – or already had – grandkids. By ending their lives he was depriving them of time they might be able to spend with their families. One such woman called Silvia, he'd got so far down the line with – had gone back to her place – but chickened out at the last minute, partway through the change that came over him. He'd seen a moment in time a few years down the line, where she'd actually have to take over looking after her granddaughter when her son and daughter-in-law died in a plane crash. It would give the woman a new lease of life, give her purpose and make her truly happy. Neil would not only be taking that away from her, he'd be taking away the future of that little girl as well.

He had morphed back, reining in his bloodlust – as hard as that was – and exited to the sound of Silvia's high-pitched screams. It was sloppy behaviour like this that had put the hunters on his tail in the first place. People like those brothers – one a little older than the other; he'd barely escaped with his life after they'd come after him and it had taken quite a while to shake them off. Then there was that guy in Holland who claimed he was some kind of descendent of quite a famous Professor – and there was Neil thinking he was just a made up character. But the worst had been that 'league' of hunters which he'd first come across in the States, and had been tracking him for quite a while now. Relentless, organised and thorough, once they had his scent it had taken a lot of ducking and diving to evade them; even now he wasn't sure he had.

He couldn't really blame them, he supposed. Neil had been a bit of a menace back there for a while. But he'd also spent a lot of time on the road just helping people as well. Went through a phase of being like the Fugitive or the Incredible Hulk (from TV series, not the later CG version), or even the Littlest – or maybe that should be the Biggest? – Hobo. The last one was probably most apt, given his unique abilities…or affliction, whichever way you wanted to look at it. Perhaps thinking he could make up for all the shit he'd done, he'd tried to help people on his way – often attempting to put his particular skills to good use, like when he took out those crooks who were putting pressure on a community with their protection racket. He'd definitely been doing the residents of that town, not to mention the world, a favour when he ripped through them.

Yet there had been times, especially lately,

when he'd thought about simply ending it all. Even had the pills laced with silver in his stuff, which he was planning to wash down with a single malt if he got low enough. Neil knew that he would live a lot longer than any human, that his chances of ending up in some kind of home were slim – he wouldn't want to die in somewhere like that anyway. A fucking werewolf in a nursing home? It was like that movie where Elvis was battling a mummy in there or something. Better to go out the way he wanted, *his* choice and his alone. It hadn't come to that yet, but it was around this time he began thinking about returning 'home'. Maybe he was winding down? Maybe he wanted to? Or maybe he was still hiding, as Kev had said – just in plain sight this time, in the last place anyone would think to look for him.

Kev had said something else, but Neil hadn't caught it; he'd been miles away. 'Hmm?'

'I said,' Kev breathed out with a sigh – Neil couldn't tell whether he was pissed off at having to repeat himself or it was his condition – 'you back to see family or something?'

The only family that had lived here were his wife and unborn child, thought Neil. His parents – the ones he'd known about anyway – had passed away a long time ago. He hadn't even bothered to return to this country when he discovered this, hadn't been particularly close with them. His real parents remained a mystery, even after doing some digging. Neil sometimes wondered if he would have gotten on better with them than he had the man and woman who'd adopted him. Maybe they'd have understood him a little better, especially his wanderlust. It made no difference now, he guessed. Remembering Kev had asked him another question and was still waiting, he shook his head.

'Just passing through, thought I'd drop in and visit.'

Kev nodded, knowing that Neil was lying – he could tell, not only from Kev's expression but from his scent again. The landlord hadn't spent all this time chatting to punters without being able to tell when someone was bullshitting him. So he left it at that, left Neil to find a table and enjoy his bitter in peace. It was obvious this customer wasn't into the conversation, so why bother?

Neil sat down in the same seat he had the night of the reunion, after Owen had brought them all back together – or at least the ones who were still okay – little realising he'd sealed the rest of their fates. Led the killer that was apparently after them right to the others in their old pack. More memory ghosts floated before him now from a Friday night similar to this one, Luke sitting opposite with his drink and Owen striding in, looking every inch the cop he'd become. He'd laid out what was happening, how Jack and Adrian were already dead, that there was someone picking them off. They'd waited for Ryan to arrive, but of course he never had – knocked down by that same killer, left to die in a hospital bed.

He closed his eyes, blinking away the spirits – and finished up his pint quickly.

Neil had other places to pay his 'respects' to.

*

If the town was dead in the daytime, then at night – and especially at the weekend – it truly came alive. If anything, the nightlife here was even better than it had been when Neil was young.

He'd heard the youth of today, in this country, still had plenty of disposable income – where they came by this, he didn't have a clue; grants and benefits probably – and it looked to him like they were intent on spending every last penny of it on a good time. As he nosed his car around the club district he'd known so well long ago, he noticed that, like the hotel he was staying in, the names of these places might have changed – from Harry's, Monty's and The Green Room, to Shapers, All Pink and The Octopus – but what was going on outside, what was spilling out onto the street, was exactly the same…maybe even worse.

At least in his day the girls didn't try and keep up with the boys in the laddish department. Neil saw young women, wearing virtually nothing at all, tumbling out of clubs and crawling around in the gutters. As he passed one, her blue hair being held back out of her face by mates, she was throwing up for England, body jerking with each fresh heave. It wasn't even that late, either. Things hadn't really started to get…interesting until after eleven when he and the guys used to frequent these kinds of places. The sights he was seeing now made him feel just as sick…and *even* older than he had before, if that was possible.

Fed up with all this, he found the side street he was looking for and headed down it. Neil parked the car and walked down the alley. His hands were shaking as he recalled the last time he'd been here, saw the man who'd killed his friends, his wife and son – older than Neil back then, but actually a good ten years younger than he was now. Not a hunter, just a father looking for revenge because *they'd* murdered his fifteen year-old daughter, Tammy, back when they were young. The irony being that was the night Neil had quit to try and make a life for himself with Julie, to settle down.

Cosmic. Fucking. Joke.

He saw the fight now, replayed it in his mind – and projected it in front of him as if he was watching a movie of what had happened over two decades ago. Neil transforming and leaping down, being hit with a silver bolt which he removed (quickly enough it didn't kill him, but not so quickly to prevent his left shoulder aching fiercely now, especially in the damp and the cold, and for the full range of movement in that arm to be impeded when in human form), the chains, tearing into the top of the man's car, then tearing into the man himself... Why hadn't he just done what Neil told him and got out of there?

Because he didn't care if he lived or died, came the answer. Just wanted to avenge his Tammy, maybe even wanted to be with her again? Fathers and their daughters, it was a complicated relationship, but there were few bonds stronger. Neil wondered how strong his bond would have been with his son, had he lived, had this man not taken the child away from him. He'd never know...just one more regret in a lifetime of them.

The scene segued into the night that had led to all this, the gang stumbling out of a club with Tammy – hair blonde, then strawberry blonde, switching between the young girl's face and Julie's, the main reason Neil didn't want to be involved with this kill. None of them had any idea she was so young, or perhaps his friends just hadn't cared... Their scenting abilities weren't nearly as honed as they would be in their forties, and a fraction of Neil's now that he was seventy. If they had been better then…

It really was true what they said, and a cliché for a reason, but youth *was* actually wasted on the young.

Neil watched, gazing open-mouthed, as the four friends began their attack, unable to do anything to prevent it. Then suddenly it dawned on him. Four…there were four guys here, and even if you didn't count Neil – as these ghosts were from his point of view – then there would still have been five of them: Adrian, Ryan, Owen, Luke and Jack. And, with that realisation, came a shift in perspective. At first glance, a couple of these boys looked a little like Adrian and Jack – but now he looked more closely, Neil saw that they weren't his late friends at all. And the other two looked nothing at all like either Owen, Luke, Ryan, or indeed himself. For one thing, these boys were a lot younger than he and his friends had been when they'd taken Tammy's life from her. Barely out of university, if they'd even gone there at all – that was another difference in this day and age, fewer kids were going to uni because of the expenses they'd incur. Or simply because they couldn't be bothered.

Neil realised that he was still standing and staring, frozen not in the past but in the present. History was repeating itself right in front of his eyes – he sniffed, getting their scent. Knowing they were near to the change, could no more control this than they could their other skills. The bloodlust coming on them. Above, the brand new full moon shone brightly and illuminated the scene. Even without his sense of smell, Neil could see who was the most important member of this pack. It wasn't Lewis (who worked part-time for the local scrap merchant), the one who had hold of a girl called Alice, not really – even though at first glance it might seem that way, because he was the leader at the moment. It wasn't Pierce, Lewis' 'second-in-command' (who stacked shelves in a supermarket just outside town); wasn't even Rav (living on benefits at the minute, but beavering away on his comic-book art), who should probably *be* the second because of the way he was holding himself.

It was a lad called Troy. He was the Neil of this pack, he was the glue that held them together, and would wrench them apart if he ever decided to leave it. He was hanging back, hesitating…and there was something about the way he was looking at Alice, pulling a strange face. He was wearing a blue shirt, jeans hanging down past his waist as the fashion seemed to demand – and his dark hair was gelled so that it looked like a wave on his head…for now, as it would definitely get messed up when the transformation took hold. Already their eyes were taking on that red and yellow cast, causing Alice – who had probably only come into this back alley with one of the group – to open her mouth and scream. Her cries were immediately absorbed by the thumping techno-beat of the nightclubs behind them.

He should just walk away and leave them to it, leave this girl to her fate… Only when he'd inhaled, Neil had also caught a whiff of her future, of what might have been – what might *yet be* if she…if Alice survived this. A lifetime of events: studying to be a lawyer; falling in love with several guys – some idiots, one complete bastard, but one kind man who stuck; a wedding; two children, one of each; an old age on her own after her husband died, but with grandchildren to love and care for, just like Silvia. Moreover, Neil also saw the possible outcome of what would happen if they did kill her, a replay of what had happened to him and his friends – not exactly the same, but close enough to send a chill down his spine.

Close enough for him to do something about it this time.

Neil was changing even before he started moving forward, his breathing controlled, feeling every single hair – the change not brought on by excitement or the smell of fear or blood, but sheer will. It was the same will that was masking his scent from them right now, allowing him the element of surprise. All four of the lads were changing too (Troy last, he noted) faster then Neil could manage but it was out of their influence; they were simply letting the beast free to do what it wanted. Neil could direct his talents where they were needed, could predict their movements – because he'd made exactly the same ones at their age.

His first task was to get Alice away from Lewis before he had a chance to sink his teeth into her throat, before he could pass her round so they could all take a bite, like she was one of those burgers Adrian used to flip in the fast food joint. If he was lucky, Neil could do this with minimal injuries to both parties. A slash at the lad's side was enough to spin him around, cause his grip to loosen on Alice. But instead of running, as she should have done, Neil buying her precious moments to get herself out of there, she just continued to scream.

By which time Lewis had turned to swipe at this newcomer, quite obviously after their prey – or so he, wrongly, assumed. Neil dodged his clumsy attack, but where he had strategy and finesse on his side, these kids had speed and strength. They weren't worn out from long years of transformation after transformation.

And there were four of them…

Lewis' second, Pierce, a lighter, orangey fur rippling across his skin, was coming to his leader's aid – as was Rav, though he was sensibly holding back a little. Somewhere in that wolf's mind was probably the thought that if Lewis and Pierce got trounced he could easily slip into the role of leader himself.

Behind him was Troy, hesitantly bringing up the rear.

Neil bent and rolled Lewis over his back, standing and tossing his opponent into the far wall, growling in satisfaction when he heard the crunch of bone and explosion of air. Pierce's attack was just as furious, but also lacked thought – allowing Neil to sidestep it easily, to follow through with a back-slash which sent him sprawling to the ground. The first setback came when Rav accidentally clawed Neil's shoulder, hitting his weak spot without even knowing it – though he quickly realised when Neil let out a howl of pain.

Alice seemed to be waking up slowly, shaking her head and realising that once the distraction was over and done with she'd be on the menu again, back in the position she'd been before this interloper came along. Neil couldn't really blame her for being in such a daze; apart from the fact that she'd just seen four young guys turn into ferocious animals right in front of her, with another, silver-furred beast wading into the mix, she had to get over the 'push', as ham-fisted as it clearly had been. Good looking as Lewis was, he'd also had help with his conquest, releasing pheromones she couldn't resist, making her susceptible to suggestion. So that when he said to her in the club, 'You fancy coming out back with me?' it had seemed like the best idea in the entire world.

Now it seemed like the absolute worst, and Alice made a break for it.

Rav was coming at Neil harder now, swiping wildly. These four also had the advantage that they weren't pulling their punches, unlike Neil. They intended to maim, hopefully *kill* their opponent. Grunting, Neil grabbed Rav's wrists and head-butted him, sending the younger wolf reeling.

That left Neil facing Troy...

They looked at each other for a moment, trying to weigh one another up – Neil having more success because of his experience. Then Troy snarled, obviously deciding it was attack or *be* attacked. He lurched forward, and Neil shadowed him, like Groucho doing the mirror routine; it seemed to throw the lad completely. But not for long. Thinking on his feet, Troy fell to all fours and then shot upwards, catching Neil under the chin and knocking him backwards. Troy continued up into the air, grabbing a nearby drainpipe and using it to swing round again.

Neil shook his head to clear it, by which time both Pierce and Rav were on their feet – and on Neil. On his back to be precise, claws digging into his sides and – in the case of Rav – his shoulder again. Though it galled him to do so, Neil resorted to trying to shake them off, like a dog coming out of the sea. It worked with Pierce, but Rav held on for grim death – which he seemed determined to cause. Seeing no other way to dislodge him, Neil backed up into the wall at speed, the pain in his shoulder incredible.

Rav struck the brickwork with a thud, and Neil felt the grip on him lessen. Then Rav slid away as Neil took a step or two forwards. He caught Troy looking at him again, but then their attention was drawn to the throng that was gathering at the head of the alley, Alice's screams now attracting a crowd, albeit of drunken revellers.

None of them needed telling: as reckless as the original quartet of werewolves had been, even they didn't want to stick around to perform for an audience. Neil had already ducked back into the shadows, observing as Pierce and Rav helped Lewis up and virtually carried him away. Troy trailed after them, gathering up torn clothes as he did so, looking over his shoulder only once at the scene – at Neil.

Wincing, Neil collected the remnants of his own clothing and receded even further into the shadows, to double back in the direction of his car, skirting the growing number of people who were flocking to a much calmer Alice. A girl who was incapable of explaining exactly had happened to her, and probably never would be able to…especially as Neil had dosed her with his own pheromones before she escaped, ones designed to fog her memory more effectively than any spiked drink could.

When he reached his vehicle, transforming back into human form, he dug around in the shredded clothing for his keys and gave a silent thanks that they were still there. He unlocked the door, dragged it open and fell inside, breathing hard. It had been a good while since he'd been in a fight that intensive, and certainly not with his own kind. With young pups who had so much energy. It had been impetuous, stupid even, but he'd felt compelled to get involved.

As he slumped back in the seat, Neil was beginning to wish he hadn't.

*

When he woke up the next morning, having entered the hotel late the previous night – he always kept a change of clothes in the car, but had to explain the bruises and bleeding to the receptionist by simply saying 'Rough night' – Neil was still of the same opinion. He should have kept his nose out of their business, let things run their course.

It was the way of the world, wasn't it? You make your mistakes, you have to live with them – he'd done that, others should be allowed the same 'opportunity'. That was just life. But at the same time, wasn't it also normal for the older generation to try and stop the younger one from making those same mistakes, to try and pass on the benefit of their wisdom…

Yeah, right, and what kind of wisdom was it said I had to get into a scrap with that generation?

he said to himself, as he sat up in bed and regretted it immediately. The mornings after a transformation weren't the easiest to recover from at the best of times now, but after what he'd been through the previous evening his whole body felt like one giant toothache. Yes it was true that they recovered faster than normal folk, but it had slowed up in the last couple of decades – hell, in the last forty years... Neil didn't want to think about that. How on earth had he done this day after day in his teens during the cycle? Let alone experienced virtually no after-effects the next morning?

He looked at the clock on the bedside table, grateful that he'd had the presence of mind to hang a 'do not disturb' on the door handle outside; he could hear the maids in other rooms, busying themselves with cleaning out baths and changing bedding. Almost half the day had been wiped out already, and he had to force himself upright, each step towards the sink in the small en-suite an effort, the clothes he'd discarded catching in his toes.

Neil turned on the light and shielded his eyes from the glare – the curtains were drawn in the main part of the room. He pulled a face when he saw the reflection, the old man staring back at him looking much older than usual. Then his face creased up even more when he took in the state of his torso, and especially his shoulder. That kid Rav had really done a number on him there, the claw marks having healed over but still angry-looking and – he suspected, because of the damage the silver had already done there – now permanent fixtures on an already-ravaged frame. Ravaged by other scars, the stories of which he had nobody to share with, and ravaged by time.

Experimentally, he raised his arms and almost let out a scream as loud as Alice's from last night – before biting his lip, remembering the maids.

Shouldn't have gotten involved, he reminded himself. But now he was….

Neil hung his head and sighed. Now that he was, he had to see it through to the end.

No matter what that meant.

*

What it meant initially, was tracing one or all of the 'cubs' he'd engaged last night. He had been in no condition to follow them the previous night – probably wasn't now, if the truth be told – but also they'd have been in no mood to listen. All that would have happened was that Neil would eventually have run out of steam and had his arse handed to him.

Maybe, though, in the cold light of day and with no danger of a transformation until it was dark, he might be able to get through to them – explain why what they were doing was so very dangerous. Try to get them to see they were drawing far too much attention to themselves…(*And who was it who let Alice go, Neil?* he said to himself. *Whose fault was it really that the crowd started to gather?*)…that what they did in the present could have a knock on effect in their futures? Futures they probably couldn't even imagine, and didn't give a shit about. At that age, the next month, or week, was like a lifetime away.

Even so, he had to try. Apart from anything else, Neil felt bad about how they'd left it last night, about the damage he'd done (*they did their fair share of damage as well, don't forget!*). So he decided to start with the one he'd felt the most connection with: Troy.

Hadn't been hard to sniff out his trail, to track him to that estate on the outskirts of town. Neil had driven through the maze of streets, his nose differentiating between the various scents wafting in through the open window. It led him to a set of communal garages, concrete bunkers covered in graffiti, with dented metal fronts. One was open, a car poking out and jacked up at the front – a pair of legs sticking out from underneath.

Neil parked and got out of his own vehicle. The feet, which had been keeping beat to a radio by the side of them, suddenly stopped tapping when Neil closed his door. By the time he was halfway to the car, Troy had slid out from under it and was standing. He sniffed the air himself, but Neil knew he wouldn't get anything from him; wouldn't be able to detect that this was the wolf he'd been tackling the previous evening.

'You lost or somethin'?' asked Troy. It was like looking in a mirror, but a mirror from almost half a century ago. Hair dark instead of grey, face smooth rather than covered in lines, body naturally lean regardless of what he stuffed his face with, Neil was willing to bet.

Troy was wearing an old T-shirt and a pair of faded jeans with a hole in the knee, both covered in oil. It was a far cry from the gear he'd been wearing out on the town, but he still managed to make it look like some kind of designer statement.

Neil paused, shook his head. 'No...but I think you and your mates might be.'

'Me and my...' Troy took a step or two towards Neil. '*You*...but how come I couldn't—'

'Don't waste your time thinking about it. Just a little magic trick I picked up along the way.' Troy's fists were up, and he was covering the distance between them. 'There's no need for that,' Neil assured him, but the lad wasn't listening. Troy clearly thought he stood more of a chance now that neither of them were changed.

He was wrong.

The same applied today as it had last night. Troy might have youth on his side but Neil saw each swing of his fists coming and was able to step out of the way – much as it pained him to do so. On the third lunge, Neil caught him and spun him around, so that Troy landed on the tarmac. He sat there staring up at Neil, who was trying very hard not to show how much the exchange had hurt him, especially his wounded shoulder.

'I'm not here to fight,' Neil said, attempting to control his breathing. 'I'm here to talk to you.' He walked over and offered him a hand up, but was actually glad when Troy batted this away and got to his own feet.

'You put my mate in the hospital last night, fucker,' spat Troy. 'I had to dump him there.'

'Lewis,' replied Neil; it wasn't a question. Lewis was the only one he'd hurt to such an extent that he might need hospitalisation. The General probably hadn't batted an eye at such injuries; just your average Friday night brawl.

'How the fuck do you know…?' Troy began, before remembering what Neil had said before about his tricks.

'Same way as I know you're Troy, Troy.'

The lad looked at him sideways. 'Just who the fuck are you?'

'Look,' said Neil, ignoring the question. 'I'm sorry about your friend, but I had to step in.'

Troy shook his head. 'What the fuck for? You're…you *were* like us.'

Neil gave a little laugh. 'I still am,' he said, but realised how lame that sounded. He wasn't like them anymore, not really. But what he'd lost in vitality, he made up for in other ways. Then he realised, that wasn't what Troy meant. Neil wasn't spontaneous any more; he thought about the risks, the consequences.

'Then why... You didn't want the...*meat* for yourself? You let her fucking go.'

'Can't you say anything without swearing?'

'Piss off,' came the considered response.

Neil laughed again; well, he *had* asked. 'I let her go because I've been there and done that; I've seen where it leads. I saw where it was going to lead with Alice.'

Troy looked confused again, not able to understand how Neil knew the name of what he'd called the 'meat' (a word he'd seemed quite uncomfortable using). Had he known her? Had that been the reason he was trying to save her? Even if that was the case, it didn't explain how he'd known who *they* were...unless he'd been following them, snooping around?

'I can teach you it, if you like,' Neil offered. 'Some of our kind are born being able to do it, but for most it comes with age and experience. I could show you, though.'

'I don't want fucking nuffin' from you!' Troy backed away towards his mounted car and Neil took a step to follow him; they were doing the Groucho thing again apparently.

'Would you just listen for a minute, I'm trying to explain.' And not doing a very good job of it, but then Troy didn't really want to hear it. 'You can only get away with this kind of stuff for so long before it's noticed.'

'More likely to get noticed when you let the fucking prey escape,' Troy answered.

'Alice,' Neil corrected. 'And don't worry about that, I sorted it. She won't remember a thing.'

'Let me guess, another bullshit trick right? Fuck off!'

Neil carried on regardless, there was a way through to this boy – had to be. 'If you don't believe anything else I'm telling you, believe that there are people out there who like nothing better than to hunt us.'

Troy's brow creased. 'Hunters? You're talking about hunters, aren't you? Bloody urban legends,' Troy insisted.

'I've seen them,' Neil countered, his voice hardening. 'I've *fought* them.' He thought he saw something in Troy's eyes then, a flicker of…what, respect? Envy maybe? *Be careful what you wish for*, thought Neil. 'But that's not all. You make enemies in other ways. People like Alice have families – relations with long memories.'

'So fucking what? Let them come,' snapped Troy. The ignorance of youth speaking. Only somebody who had nothing to lose could say that, but only someone who'd lost it all could say:

'So…*everything*, son.'

'I'm not your shitting son,' stated Troy.

'No,' said Neil with a catch in his voice. 'My son was killed by someone who wanted that kind of justice, that kind of revenge. Somebody reacting to something I'd done when I was only a bit older than you and hadn't been thinking.'

'Good!' said the boy. Neil reduced distance between them in an instance – and without a thought for how sore he was proceeded to slap Troy across the face.

The lad reeled backwards, not from the force of the blow but purely because it was so unexpected. He reached up and touched his cheek. Neil pointed at him with a rigid finger. 'How dare you...little prick! I *know* you're not my son, and thank Christ for that! I'd be fucking ashamed of you!' There was something about Neil using that word which made Troy flinch even more than the slap had. Neil couldn't help it, he took a sniff – he 'read' Troy without really meaning to.

He saw a kid who'd basically been dragged up, whose real father – who hadn't stuck around past Troy's sixth birthday – had knocked the living shite out of him on a regular basis (the boy curling up into a protective ball), not to mention what he'd done to Troy's mum. He saw a single mother who'd tried to make ends meet by legitimate means to begin with, but had fallen into more unsavoury ways of earning a living and got drunk most nights to try and forget the fact. He saw a succession of 'boyfriends' Troy's mother had welcomed into their home – a council flat on this very estate – many of which were just as bad, if not worse than his own father. He saw bullying at school, Troy being pushed around and spat on because he never really fitted in anywhere…until he left school early at sixteen to do a course in mechanics at college (a natural, always tinkering with engines) and had met up with the rest of his pack there, bunking off and playing cards. Wasn't long after that he turned for the first time, fed for the first time – his mum's latest waste of space druggie boyfriend who pushed Troy too far after he got high one full moon… Troy's mum had been out of it, but she'd seen the blood the next morning. She hadn't said much about it, hadn't said much at all before she'd overdosed one night when Troy was out. Neil saw him dropping out of college, earning his way by fixing cars on the sly, which was what he was still doing today…

Saw him in some basement somewhere, naked and shackled with silver manacles, two men with baseball caps using torture implements constructed from the same material to make him scream. Just like Alice had screamed.

Hunters. Those same hunters Troy insisted were mythical.

'I…I'm sorry,' said Neil under his breath. He wasn't sure himself whether he was apologising for the slap, or saying how sorry he was about Troy's crappy life. Maybe a little of both.

Troy found his voice from somewhere. 'What the fuck, man! Just what the fuck!' Again, what the fuck was Neil doing there in the first place? What the fuck was the slap all about? What the fuck...just what the fuck? Neil was beginning to wonder himself.

'I'm sorry,' was all he could manage again.

'Just get the fuck away from me, man. Get the fuck out of here and leave me and my friends alone.'

Neil opened his mouth to say something, then nodded. But as he was walking away from the scene, he called back over his shoulder. 'Just to let you know, I'll be around tonight in town...so maybe you and your friends should take a rain check.' He wasn't sure how much of a threat that was, how much of a threat *he* was, but Neil hoped at least it would give Troy something to think about, something to tell his friends about. There really was no point trying to talk to them if he couldn't get through to Troy; they'd be just as stubborn, probably more.

So Neil got back into his car, turned it around.

He watched the boy through his rear view mirror, standing next to the car he'd been fixing. Neil watched Troy, just as Troy was watching Neil drive away. A thought passed through his mind. That they were two opposite ends of the spectrum – young and old. But also opposite ends of the story, the beginning…

And the end.

*

Neil thought about what he'd said, later, when he was driving. 'I'll be around in town tonight.' On the streets, patrolling, like he was Batman or something.

If he was, then surely he'd have a better car than this one. Didn't matter, it was getting the job done, getting him about. He'd been going in circles for a while now with the window open, sifting through the myriad of scents to see if Troy or any of his mates were on the prowl in town tonight. Wasn't easy, it was even busier than Friday night – which was probably only to be expected – but Neil prided himself on such skills.

Eventually, he left the car behind and pounded the pavements, checking the back alleys on foot. He wasn't about to venture into any of the pubs or clubs; if he was too old back in his forties to be seen in them, then he'd definitely draw attention to himself now. 'Hey granddad, move it or lose it!' 'Don't do your hip in on the dance floor!' 'Post office is closed if you're looking to get your pension.'

Though it was tempting to *change* and patrol that way – it would be quicker to get around and his aches and pains had more or less gone by now – he resisted. The moon glared down at him, accusingly. How dare he refuse the gift it was offering? It was safer this way, though: oh, he could control himself when in wolf form most of the time, but there was just too much temptation here for his liking. When he was changed, his bored animal brain might just whisper to him: *Go on, what harm would it do, really? It's not like you haven't done it before.* How ironic would it be for him to be out here trying to prevent that from happening, only to fall off the wagon himself?

Neil saw the pair in the alley now, messing about, a particularly amorous couple who'd gone back there for a bit of privacy. He observed them from the shadows, devouring each other in a different way altogether, drunk and excited by the fact they might be caught at any moment. It reminded him of the first few months with Julie, how they'd been together, unable to keep their hands off each other...and that last time, after the reunion, *both* of them like wild animals in bed. He'd never have that again. Before he could help himself, there was a tear rolling down his cheek which he wiped away with the back of his hand.

Teeth gritted, he'd let out a growl then which echoed up the alleyway, causing the couple to stop. They'd looked in his direction, at each other, then started pulling their clothes back on and stumbled off – terrified. That had made him feel a little better, but afterwards he'd felt guilty for acting so childishly.

He'd come across nothing else, however, and called it a night in the wee small hours of the morning, heading back to his hotel room to crash for a couple of hours' sleep. Neil was happy that his words seemed to have sunk in with Troy – or at the very least that none of the young pups wanted to encounter him again.

A couple of hours turned into several, and once again he was glad he'd left the 'do not disturb' sign on his door handle. Blinking wearily, Neil saw that it was after midday. He lay back on the pillow, groaning. Then he reached for the remote control and switched on the TV, searching through the channels for something that wasn't country-related or religious (it *was* Sunday). He settled for the local news, which he watched for a few moments before deciding it was too depressing and muted it, wandering off into the bathroom to pee. He was just about to begin when he saw the reflection in the mirror – not his own, but familiar all the same. On the TV. A young girl he'd seen the night before last.

'Alice?' said Neil under his breath. He rushed back into the main room and snatched up the remote, quickly pressing the mute button again and catching the end of the report.

'...missing now since yesterday. Alarms were raised when she failed to show up at her parents' home for an anniversary dinner. Once again, if anyone has any information about the disappearance of missing Alice Timberland then could you please ring…'

The newsreader continued on, but Neil wasn't really listening. He was thinking about Alice, about how it couldn't really be a coincidence that she'd vanished. In his experience there weren't such things as coincidences like this. Neil was thinking that one of the young wolves had done it, maybe because they were frightened of her saying something about Friday night – or simply because they were too proud to let the 'meat' escape.

He ground his teeth together, even gave a little snarl.

It was time to have another word with Troy, probably with the rest of them as well. Before tonight, preferably.

Before the third and final night of the full moon.

*

Troy wasn't at the garage today, but Neil had very little trouble tracking him down from there.

He found him on a nearby stretch of scrubland, watching a makeshift football match. Troy, this time wearing trackies, was standing with a bunch of people on the sidelines – with them, but quite obviously not *with* them. They were following the passage of the ball from one end of the field to the other, where the player with it would try and kick the thing through a goal made from jumpers. The more things change, the more they stay the same, Neil thought – recalling matches just like this when he was growing up; kids making their own entertainment.

It had been an age since he'd seen football live, and before he realised Neil soon found himself watching the game too, getting caught up in it, trying to figure out who was playing against whom – it was harder than it looked when they didn't have differently coloured shirts on, plus allegiances appeared to keep changing all the time. Troy seemed to be able to decipher it all, though, and gave a cheer when the goal was finally scored. It was only now, when he turned, that he spotted Neil.

He thought for a moment Troy was going to bolt, make a run for it just as Alice had finally done when she'd been freed. In the end he remained where he was, perhaps reasoning that it would draw too much attention to himself. Maybe the people here would think the cops were after him, and word would spread. How many folk would bring their cars to him for fixing then? Neil was glad he didn't run, as he wasn't sure he'd be able to keep up with him – keep him in sight – let alone catch him.

Once he was certain Troy wasn't going anywhere, Neil approached and inserted himself into the crowd. 'What the fuck do *you* want?' Troy whispered; in fact he was barely speaking, but knew Neil would be able to hear.

'A word,' Neil whispered back through gritted teeth.

'Got nothin' to say to you.'

Neil produced something from behind his back, then turned and slapped it into Troy's chest. It was a local paper he'd picked up from the hotel foyer, folded at the moment. Puzzled, Troy opened it up, looking left and right to see if anyone had noticed. Neil couldn't work out whether it was the act itself the lad was worried about, or the fact he might be seen holding a newspaper. The paper was already on the page Neil had been reading, and that was the first thing Troy saw after he'd unfolded it.

'The fucking meat,' Troy mouthed when he spotted the photo accompanying the piece on page four.

'Call her by her name, Troy. She's not meat, she's not prey.' At that moment the football was kicked over in their direction. Neil stopped it by trapping it under his foot, then – without even looking – he kicked it back into the middle of the players, who shouted their thanks. He continued: 'I saw the way you were looking at her on Friday night, you know that yourself.' Or at the very least Troy was on his way to figuring it out. 'Call her by her name.'

'Alice,' said Troy, a bit too loudly.

'So, still got nothing to say to me?' Neil took him by the arm, but Troy wrenched it away. Then he looked at Neil and nodded, began to walk off from the match with his escort close beside him.

Once they were far enough from other people to talk, Troy spun around and repeated, 'It wasn't me…it wasn't fucking me,' over and over, like some kind of disciple of Shaggy's.

'I believe you,' said Neil. 'I'd know if you were lying anyway.'

'When you left yesterday I got in touch with Rav and Pierce, told them what you'd said, told them you were a fucking headache. They agreed it was better to lay low at the moment, at least this month.'

'That's what they *told* you,' said Neil. 'But obviously one of them had other ideas. Did you tell them I fixed it, that she wasn't going to tell anyone?'

Troy nodded.

'And they believed you? I'm not even sure you believed me.'

'Man, it wasn't fucking them either. I was Pixchatting them last night, they were both at home.'

'What the hell's Pixchatting?' asked Neil.

Troy got out his phone, a smartphone, the kind Neil hated; what did he need one for, anyway? He had nobody he needed or wanted to keep in touch with. And somehow, while his back was turned, mobiles had transformed into things that connected you to social media sites or had facile games on them that turned the users into zombies. Troy showed him the

Pixchat app which, as far as Neil could see, involved taking pictures of yourself or the things around you and adding lines of dialogue to them in an effort to have some kind of inane conversation (in this instance a lot of derogatory remarks about Neil). Didn't anyone simply talk on the phone anymore?

Nevertheless, Neil could see the timestamps next to Pierce and Rav's faces; could see that the 'chat' went on periodically most of the night; could see the background of their houses, the pictures of their TVs, walls and whatever that marked them as being at home, just as Troy had testified.

'See?'

Neil shook his head. He didn't trust this modern technology, and still didn't believe in coincidences. 'Get your friends together, I want to meet with you all.'

Now it was Troy's turn to shake his head. 'They won't fucking go for it, man!'

Neil grabbed his arm again, this time harder than before – but when he saw the fear in the boy's eyes, saw the memories reflected there of his father, he let go again. 'This is serious, Troy. It's a big deal for a place like this. The police are looking into it already.'

Troy held up a hand. 'All right, all right...*where* do you want to meet them, then?'

'Where all this began,' Neil said without missing a beat. 'And where it's going to finish.'

*

The alleyway looked very different in daylight.

Neil and Troy waited there in silence for a while, his friends late for the meet, but then the quiet grew uncomfortable.

'I'm not the enemy, you know,' Neil ventured, leaning back against the wall – looking across the way at Troy sitting on a fire escape, his legs dangling down.

'Could've fooled me,' the youth said. 'Must've been someone else who got stuck into us on Friday, then?'

Neil hung his head. 'I've explained about that. I had to do it. I could see where it was heading.'

'Yeah, you fucking said.'

'It's only because I've gone through all this that—'

'But that was you. Newsflash: *I'm* not you.

My friends aren't fucking *you*.'

'No, that's true...but, believe it or not, there are definite similarities to me and my old mates. There always are in life.'

'Did they have an old fogy on *their* backs complaining about what they were doing?'

Neil shook his head. 'But I wish someone *had* spoken to us back then...because my friends might still be alive now if somebody had done what I'm doing.'

'Right, and of course you'd have listened,' said Troy sarcastically. 'But hey, why don't you just travel back in time and fix it all, I mean you can do everything fucking else. Magic, like you said.'

Neil sighed. 'Trust me, if I could, I would.'

'All that Jedi bollocks, all that knowing everything and seeing into the future. Fucking give me a break.'

'I'm *trying* to give you a break, Troy.' The lad muttered something, but he didn't ask what it was. Just the same old crap. 'Look, I get it – I understand what you've been through, and why you're so defensive but—'

Troy scowled. 'You don't know shit about me.'

'I do actually,' Neil said, with a certainty in his voice. 'You said it yourself, the Jedi bollocks.'

The lad shook his head. 'You don't...don't know shit,' he repeated, but there was less conviction this time. A silence settled between them which, surprisingly, Troy broke. 'Was that true, what you said to me yesterday?'

'Was what true?' asked Neil.

'What you said about...about your son, about the hunters?'

Neil gave a single nod. 'It was the road you were going down as well. I saw it. And Alice was the key. *Was* being the operative word.'

'I told you man, it—'

'Wasn't you, I know.'

'And it wasn't Pierce or Rav.'

Neil folded his arms. 'I'd like to hear that from their lips. No offence.'

Troy shrugged.

'So maybe you should just come out and we can get this over and done with,' Neil said with a smirk.

'How the fuck...' came a voice from some distance away. Rav, hiding round the side of the building, revealed himself, dragging Pierce with him. Now, in the light, Neil got a better look at them both. Rav's dark skin, his stance like some kind of ancient Prince. Pierce's washed-out look, the ginger hair topping it off. They ventured down the alley, but kept a reasonable distance between themselves and Neil.

'Look, he's just an old man,' Rav pointed out.

'An old man who was beating the crap out of you the other night,' Neil replied.

'How about we try that again right now, then?' Rav was sneering.

'Ready when you are,' Neil answered him. It was the bluster and bravado of youth versus the confidence of age. He'd learned a long time ago that even if you weren't particularly confident, if you appeared it then that was half the battle – especially in a pissing contest.

'Guys…it's okay, he just wants to talk,' Troy assured them. 'It's about the girl from the other night, Alice.'

'Our meal,' Pierce corrected, running a tongue over his lips. He pointed at the older man: 'The one you made us miss out on.'

'Maybe. Maybe not,' Neil said. 'She's

missing, and it's been noticed.'

'What's that got to do with us?' asked Rav, touching his chest.

'I think one of you followed her, went to finish the job.' Neil stated.

Rav and Pierce exchanged looks, then said almost as one: 'Wasn't us.'

Neil sniffed the air. Even if he didn't trust the photos on Troy's phone, he did trust his own senses: they were telling the truth. So where did that leave them?

'Wait a second,' said Rav. 'Has anyone heard from Lewis?'

All three of them shook their heads. 'Not since the hospital,' Troy admitted. 'I just assumed he was still there.'

'You don't think...' Pierce was looking to Troy for answers. Suddenly it had become their conversation, these three friends.

'Naw...he was pretty fucking out of it when I left him,' Troy told them, looking over at Neil. The transformation back to human wouldn't have helped with the injuries, that's for sure. They were in a more vulnerable state then.

'But we do heal faster than other people,'

Neil reminded him, trying to convince himself. It wasn't inconceivable that Lewis had gone in search of that which had been denied him. After all, he'd put in the groundwork. And then, when he was stronger, maybe he'd come after Neil. But wouldn't he have included the rest of his pack in his plan? Wasn't there safety in numbers?

Still...

Rav had his phone out, was tapping away on the screen. 'Just texted him.'

Neil sighed. 'Can't you just ring him up?'

They looked at him blankly. 'We could send him a FaceSpace message,' Pierce suggested. It would appear that unless they happened to be in the vicinity, this generation would much prefer 'speaking' via words on a screen. But it struck Neil that as connected as they were, these people really couldn't be further apart; they hadn't even bothered to find out how Lewis was since he'd been dumped at the hospital. And *Neil* couldn't be further apart from them.

He went over to Troy and demanded the boy hand over his phone so he could call Lewis. 'No fucking way, man!' They were also apparently the most precious things these youngsters possessed. Neil turned and strode over to Rav instead, snatching the phone out of his hand.

'*Hey!*' he shouted, reaching for it back.

'Leave him, he won't be able to fucking work it out anyway,' said Pierce. 'Look at him.'

As much as he hated to admit it, Neil was struggling with the workings of the thing in his hand. The last time he'd used a mobile, they'd actually had buttons on the front, numbers you simply pressed to dial. He heard sniggering coming from the trio, and threw the phone back at Rav – who fumbled but caught it. 'Shithead!'

'*Ring him!*' Neil barked. 'Get him here!'

Rav glared at him, but eventually did as he was told, looking down at the screen and tapping things into it, doing what Neil had been unable to: finding Lewis' number and dialling.

He was in the process of bringing up the phone to his ear when Rav suddenly paused, shuddered, then let it go – let it clatter to the floor. That made no sense, not when he'd been so angry about Neil's mistreatment of the thing. Then the boy staggered forward a couple of steps, looking down at his chest where a bloom of red had appeared. He touched it, bringing his fingers up to a confused face, before his eyes rolled into his head and he collapsed face-first onto the ground.

'Shit!' said Neil, then to Pierce: 'Take cover!' The ginger kid was still trying to work out what had happened to his mate, but Neil already knew. '*Get down!*' Pierce just stood there, like Alice had done when they were attacking her; it was only when another bullet pinged off the floor behind him that he started to get his arse in gear, to shift sideways.

Neil was sniffing the air, but getting nothing. He wasn't the only one who could mask his scent apparently. A spark hit the alley wall not far from his head and he lunged across, towards Troy and the fire escape.

'W-What's happening?' he asked.

'You know those hunters that don't exist,' shouted Neil. 'Well, they're here.'

Troy's face was white as Neil joined him on the platform. 'No...it can't—'

Neil took his face in his hands. 'Listen to me, I need you to focus – they've come for us in the day because they think it's safe. Because they think we can't change.'

Troy was simply staring at him.

'But we can! You just need to concentrate. It's not dark yet, but we're still in the cycle. The moon's up there, you just have to connect with—' A bullet pinged off the fire escape; they were shooting from a rooftop somewhere. Neil squinted, his eyesight not perfect but good enough to trace the trajectory of the projectile. He let out a growl, then breathed in, closed his eyes. Maybe if Troy saw it for himself, he'd believe... Another little trick Neil had picked up over the years, though more a realisation, really. They all were.

Neil reached out and began to feel it, the power of the sphere up there – the pumping of the blood in his veins, hairs just waiting to push up through his skin. He knew his eyes were changing because of Troy's reaction, a mixture of surprise and awe. Now, when he looked down at himself, Neil saw that change – shirt and trousers being replaced by fur, muscles bulging as he readied himself.

Then he was away, up the fire escape, dodging another bullet that ricocheted off the struts. He was angry and it fuelled his actions, helping him to claw his way to the top of the building and bound onto it. Neil spotted the sniper almost immediately, one rooftop away – but he could cover that distance easily enough. The man had his long hair tied back in a ponytail, out of his eyes – one of which was pressed against a scope on top of his rifle. There was a long extension on the end of this, a silencer so that they'd have no warning at all. Still there was no scent to him, as close as Neil was – some kind of blocker-cream perhaps?

Now the man saw him, rose from his position and swung the rifle in Neil's direction as the wolf leapt across the gap. Neil angled himself sideways, so that the silent bullet – obviously silver – whipped past. The man was swearing in a language Neil didn't recognise, cursing and firing another shot that missed its mark. He dropped the larger weapon in favour of a handgun he drew out of the back of his dark jeans. Holding it straight, he let off a succession of shots that were also dulled by a silencer. Neil dodged left and right, before finally crouching then springing forward to savage the guy. He ripped into him, biting and clawing, tearing into him before lifting him off the roof and tossing him down into the alley itself.

The blood told him all he needed to know about these people, even before he saw the van pull up at the head of the passageway. The league... Neil let out a howl of despair. Down in the alley, more armed men were pouring out of the vehicle, some wearing caps; one pulled a gun on Pierce and shot him in the head, in the eye to be precise; blood and brains exploded out of the back of his skull. Trained and professional, these men were also cowards – expecting to face their quarry in a weakened state.

And then there was Troy, who hadn't really moved from his position on the fire escape. He had his eyes closed, body curled up into a ball – terrified, paralysed with fear. Neil had no choice: he had to get down there as quickly as possible.

He ran to the edge of the rooftop and jumped.

Neil felt the rush of wind as he speeded up, plummeting into the alley. His aim was as good as the shooter he'd just taken out, landing on one of the men, pushing his shoulders down into his body with a crunch, but then hitting the ground awkwardly – feeling the vibrations up his legs, the bones not taking the impact well.

Now he was surrounded. One move and he'd be riddled with silver bullets.

'Alive!' came a voice – sounded American. 'Take this one alive!'

Neil paused, breathing in and out. No sudden moves. So this was how it was going to end, captured and taken to some dungeon somewhere – or maybe even sold on to some covert government agency so they could experiment on him? After so many close calls, Neil guessed he couldn't argue with that and it was probably no more than he deserved.

Then it happened. Something was moving quickly, circling the men and slashing at their hamstrings with razor-sharp claws. The first couple dropped, letting off shots into the air as they fell. Neil seized his chance and clawed at the closest man, raking up and slicing the rifle he was holding in half, then continuing on into his chin so that the claws exited at his cheeks.

More cries in foreign languages – one Polish

maybe? – as the men started to panic. Neil bit the throat out of another, as a couple more dropped to their knees – crippled by the blur that was still racing round them. He caught a glimpse of it between the figures; Troy, half-transformed, as much of a change he could muster in the daylight, but still deadly. He looked more like those old-fashioned film versions of wolfmen than a giant full-blown wolf – he still had his trackies on – but in time he'd master the process, Neil felt sure.

Between them they were taking down the shocked hunters, who'd been expecting to simply pick off these creatures in their human forms. One pulled out a silver knife and slashed at Neil, maybe hoping that close quarter combat would be better, but Neil just dodged it and wrenched off his arm.

Then Neil saw something flying through the air, heading towards them – something small and black, tossed from the van. Some kind of grenade, it would land closer to Troy than Neil…but the youth hadn't seen it.

Without even thinking, Neil dove in Troy's direction, shoving him out of the way as the black object landed and exploded. It wasn't like any kind of explosion Neil had seen before, though; there wasn't much of a flash or bang — instead the air just sparkled. And then it hit him, going in through his lungs, being absorbed through his pores.

Silver. Not a shrapnel bomb, no — this was worse than that. Particles of silver that were burning him up from the inside out. Neil let out a howl of actual pain now, his turn to curl up on the floor, coughing and spluttering.

Troy was on his knees, starting to work out what had happened. He made to move over, but Neil waved him back. The older wolf grunted, attempting to stand. They'd felled the men in the alley, but there was one still left who'd thrown the grenade. Who was emerging from the front of the van, dragging someone with him and holding a pistol to her temple.

Neil recognised the hostage immediately. It was the missing girl, Alice. She'd been beaten, had one black eye and a split lip, and she was crying.

'Yeah, you know who this is, dontchya?' said the broad-chested man, his bald head covered in sweat. He was addressing Neil, but cast a glance over at Troy as well. 'I can see that you do, monster! Saw the way you were protecting her the other night. What is she to you, some kinda relation?'

Neil just growled. She wasn't anything more to him than another ghost, a reminder of a girl he should have saved when he was younger. He'd got it all so wrong, though. The young pups weren't the ones who would bring the hunters here, he'd already done that himself – they'd trailed him from abroad. And it hadn't been Lewis who'd gone after Alice, it had been them. In fact, Lewis was probably dead, just like Pierce and Rav, and then he and Troy soon. The league was nothing if not thorough. Neil had made it easy for them, gathered those left in one place to make their task simple. More parallels.

The hunter dragged Alice forward, then removed the gun from her temple, aiming instead at Troy. 'You, I don't give a shit about. Just another dead growler, though I've never seen any who could shift in the day before. But you...' He kicked Neil in the side. 'We've been waiting a long time for this. You're gonna to come quietly with me, aintchya?'

But Neil had one last trick up his sleeve,

something they could all do but he'd refined. He didn't even have to growl. His own form of 'texting'.

When I say now, Troy – take him out...
Troy's brow furrowed, trying to work out how Neil was talking to him. But then, he'd seen – he'd *done* – stranger things that day.

Now!

Neil bit into the hunter's calf, causing him to cry out loud. His aim shifted, allowing Troy to leap straight at him. The young lycanthrope careered into the guy, and he let go of Alice – who tottered sideways like a crab, out of the way. Neil watched as Troy relieved the hunter of his firearm, then slammed him up against the side of the van.

The man gave a defiant laugh. 'Might not be today, but one day you're gonna to get yours, freak!'

You reap what you sow, thought Neil.

Then the hunter spat in Troy's face and, seconds later, he had no mouth to spit with. Troy had opened his jaw wide, locking on to his enemy's face as if Hannibal Lecter himself had given him lessons.

When he was done, he turned. Alice had

backed up into a corner of the alley, was sitting and shaking, still crying her eyes out. Neil was struggling to get up, struggling to get a breath.

Troy walked over to him, stood over him.

And then he offered him his paw.

*

The hunters hadn't been the only thing Neil had been wrong about.

It hadn't ended in that alleyway, not really. While Troy had cleaned up as best he could, eating his fill and gathering together all the weaponry that was left behind, he'd left Neil and Alice alone in the van so the old wolf could do his thing, or try to at any rate. Neil was pretty spent, each time he took a breath it hurt him, but he managed to wipe the images of the wolves from her mind again…then paused, adding something else.

They'd dropped her off a little way from the alley, putting in an anonymous call to the police using one of the mobiles, before breaking them all – even Troy's. By now they'd both changed back, and it had become clear that Neil badly needed medical attention. Not only had the silver ruined his lungs, his legs were pretty screwed from that jump. Troy left him wrapped in a blanket at the hospital gates, where he knew the man would be found, and drove off in the van – without even so much as a goodbye.

Neil only remembered bits and pieces; he'd been pretty out of it at the time.

The people in casualty did their best, stabilised Neil enough for him to be transferred to an elderly day-care facility where they could devote more time to looking after him…supposedly.

That's where Troy had found him again a week or so later, after blagging his way inside by saying he was a volunteer visitor, something they always welcomed. Neil had been propped up in bed, staring out of the window. When he'd turned to look, he'd wheezed, 'You lost or something?'

Troy had smiled at that. 'No, but I thought you were, back there… Sorry I had to bail, man, but I had to get rid of all that stuff, the van. The…well, the rest of it.'

Neil had nodded, he understood. The important thing was, Troy had returned, had actually gone out of his way to track Neil down. Just like Alice had apparently tracked Troy down.

'Found me at my garage,' he said. 'Your doing, I suppose?'

'Well, she is a pretty girl,' Neil said, then began coughing – hard. So hard, Troy asked him if he needed a nurse. Neil shook his head, and took a drag on the oxygen from the cylinder they'd left beside him. 'You…you could do a lot worse.'

'She wanted to thank me, but didn't know what for.' He laughed. 'The police think she was taken by some kind of trafficking ring, you know. That she got away… She remembers men, being manhandled.'

Neil nodded. 'All I could manage at short notice.'

'So…' said Troy, taking a seat.

'So…' managed Neil.

'So how're you doing for a start?'

'To put…to put it in language you…might understand: I'm fucking fucked. My legs are fucked and my lungs…'

Troy nodded, looked down. 'I'm sorry.'

'No need. I made a choice,' breathed out

Neil. 'But for once I don't regret it.'

'And what happens now?' Troy had asked.

'What…what happens is we talk. Y'know, the old fashioned way.'

So they did, they'd talked that day and for many more to come; sometimes out loud, sometimes not. Neil had told him his stories, tried to warn him about the pitfalls – things he should look out for as a member of this unique clan. He'd also offered him some options: to live as he had been doing, or to simply *live*. To see where things might go with Alice, if he wanted. To stay or to leave

They'd played cards – it wasn't Elvis and the Mummy, but it was nice. And Neil had shown Troy how to do a few more of those magic tricks of his, things it had taken a lifetime to learn, or at the very least set him on the path to learning. Some of it really did only come with time, with age. 'You just have to keep practising,' Neil had told him.

He'd done all this, not because he felt guilty, but because he wanted something in return. Troy had already hidden Neil's hire car away, and when they were coming to the end of their visits, he asked a favour of him. Asked him to bring something from the glove compartment, smuggle the items in.

Looking over his shoulder, Troy had passed him the pills and the flask. Neil opened it up and sniffed. 'Ah, that's the good stuff.'

'And…and you're sure this is what you want?' asked Troy. Neil wasn't certain, but he thought he saw tears in the lad's eyes.

'Yeah, I'm sure. I don't want this to drag on. I'd rather go out on my terms. One last choice.'

Troy said nothing, but Neil could see that he understood.

'You know, I once said I was glad you're not my son, but the truth is…I always sort of felt like you were. I know that's pretty odd, but—'

The boy got up and made to leave. Was a couple of steps towards the door before he stopped, turned, and went back to hug Neil. Just wrapped his arms around him. Neil hugged him too. 'You…you take care of yourself, son. Okay?'

He felt the boy nodding into his shoulder.

Then he was gone. Neil wiped the tears from his cheeks, before taking out the pills, popping one into his mouth and swallowing with a swig of whiskey.

It was time, he thought.
Finally, it was time.

*

Troy was wiping away the tears as well, as he stepped out of the day-care centre for the last time. As he made his way towards his car.

It was almost a month to the day since the old man had come into his life, since he'd exploded into it as devastatingly as the grenade that had done all the damage during their last fight. He'd sat and listened to Neil, come to think of him like a father – as bizarre as that sounded. But, like a father, he wasn't sure whether to take the man's advice or not. Whether to just go his own way, be his own man. There was no way he would make the same mess of things anyway.

Yeah, he had some decisions to make, definitely. But they were his choices and his alone.

Troy slid behind the wheel, looked up at the darkening sky. It was Friday night, a full moon. He knew Alice would be waiting for him to call her, but truth be told he was thinking about a night out. Was starting to become bored, was missing the thrum of the clubs and pubs. He was only young, when all was said and done.

And there really was nothing like a good night out, thought Troy.

Nothing like it in the world.

Another Life

All those lives, different lives.

If she cared to, and especially at this time of the month, she could see – *smell*, more accurately – the content of their days, their years, so far on this planet. But even if she couldn't, some you could tell their life-story just by looking at them, even if they weren't here on this particular night.

Take the man in the booth not far from the door, nursing his Sam Adams. Looking down into the beer, and up occasionally to scan the room – attempting to catch the eye of some female, but not confident enough to get up and ask any of them out. Probably for the best, dressed as he was. Mommy's boy, had lived with her – *looked after* her – until she'd died…fairly recently, a sniff confirmed. Father had passed away early, leaving them enough to live on, meaning the son had never had to go out to earn a living. Meaning he could devote all his time to the woman, who'd made sure his dedication to her was ingrained from an early age. It had left him with very few social skills, in fact she was surprised he was even out tonight – and at a bar like this. But then loneliness could be crippling, could be worse than physical pain sometimes.

Diana understood that better than most.

Her turn to look down into the drink that was in front of her, a vodka and tonic. The clear surface reflected her features back at her, the lines on her face more noticeable than they had been even five years ago when she was in her early forties, instead of approaching the big five-zero. The redness of her hair from a bottle now instead of the natural ginger it had been growing up and into her twenties and thirties. Oh, she was still considered a looker for her age – nowhere near some of her contemporaries, and given the life she'd led any one of them might have appeared twenty years older than they should have done. A *hard* life, that's what some would have put it down to.

She looked away, looked back across the bar

again. Searching the faces, sniffing once more – picking up the false bravado of one guy at the back who was chatting up a woman, giving it all the patter when in real life he couldn't even stand up to his boss at work. Would cry himself to sleep most nights, never having been able to keep up a relationship for very long; they'd always see right through him in no time at all. If he'd drop the bullshit and just let someone in, he'd get exactly what he wanted – a woman to spend the rest of his, admittedly pitiful, life with. Someone to share things with, to talk to. It was an itch he just couldn't scratch.

Then you had the flip side of the coin, the guys with *too much* confidence. Who targeted those of the opposite sex who had even less self-belief than the man with the chat. Who'd been through brutal, messy divorces, leaving them with no self-respect whatsoever. There was one now, homing in on a woman who was barely forty but had been through all of that and more. Been cheated on, lied to, told she was ugly – when in fact if she used half the make-up she did she'd actually be quite stunning. Make-up as a mask, a shield. Covering up who you were for a night like this. Everyone wore one, but some masks were more necessary than others.

And look, yes, already she was falling for his heavy-handed technique. He'd get what he wanted from the woman, then leave her in some hotel room feeling used and unloved, just like always.

It would serve that bastard right if Diana just—

No, not him. It would draw too much attention. Besides, he was busy anyway with his conquest. Once he'd got another couple of drinks inside her, they'd be off; sometimes he needed drugs to help…weaken their resolve, but not this time. He had it all planned out. She might not even make it to the hotel, might just end up in the back of his pick-up with her legs in the air. Maybe next time, Diana said to herself. She was good with faces, even had his name now – Wayne – his scent, and was sure she'd see him again. If she felt so inclined, would even be able to track him to the trailer where he lived, lie in wait for him to emerge and then…

Diana's gaze swept across the room again.

Singles' Night – it brought them all out. Was why she came. As much as Wayne believed himself to be a predator, he had nothing on her.

She paused, spotting the man with greying hair in the corner.

He had a different look to everyone else in here, seemed so out of place it was unreal. For a second they locked eyes, then he looked away again. Took a sip of the whiskey that was on the table in front of him. Diana sniffed. Nothing... She got nothing from him, frowned. That never happened. So what—

'...sitting here?'

The voice wrenched her from her thoughts, and as she turned to take in the fella by the side of her, Diana's frowned deepened. *Christ! It couldn't be...* She almost dropped off her stool. Then she blinked, shook her head, told herself that no, it absolutely couldn't – and indeed wasn't. But the similarity was amazing.

'Are you okay?' he asked her.

'Are you still pure?'

'I...' She turned back to look for the man in the corner, but he'd gone – and Diana faced front again, faced the man who was talking to her. 'Sorry, what?'

He ran a hand through his boot-black hair, smiled with teeth that were unnaturally white. 'I asked if anyone was sitting here.' The man gestured to the empty seat beside her, and she shook her head again. He parked one buttock on the stool, left one leg dangling. The man was wearing a white shirt and dark trousers that might have been the bottom half of a suit. 'Good. That's good.'

'That's good. I'm glad you're still pure, sweetie. Still Pop's little girl.'

It was even there in his voice. Practically the same... And now Diana found herself looking at another reflection, of a past that she herself had lived. The content of her own days and years on this planet. Though strangely she flashed back not to him, to his voice – but to *her*. The mother she'd lost so early, the opposite of the guy with the Sam Adams. A warmness, feeling safe in her embrace (one of the last times): the woman who'd named her after a goddess, told her she was special. Magical.

Then nothing but him. Her father, Roy. And that had been fine, he hadn't been a bad parent – a little on the strict side, but then what would you expect from such a deeply religious man as him? Only beat her when it was really 'necessary', or he wanted her to be quiet. He used to tell her that God had taken her mom because it was his will, and she was now up in Heaven at his side, enjoying the benefits eternal life could offer. Hadn't known her at all, though, had he? Not really.

Roy had worked at a local delivery place: good, honest grind, either behind the counter or driving parcels out to people; used to joke during the festive season that he was Father Christmas making his rounds... Or Poppa Christmas, as he called himself. It put food on the table and a roof over their heads, even if it was only a flat in their tiny hometown of Nowheresville USA.

It wasn't really until she started to grow up, until boys began taking an interest – and they were only friends from school, just buddies as they tended to be before you'd even hit ten. But that had been enough to set him off, to try and isolate her. And it had only got worse after that, moving up to High School. He'd set curfews for her, made sure she was back home straight away after lessons ended, that she was in her room doing her homework. Occasionally, out in the schoolyard, she thought she saw his delivery van go past – just keeping an eye on her, spying, making sure the boys there weren't *too* friendly.

'You know all about right and wrong,' he'd said to her on the way back from church one Sunday. 'Listen to those lessons you've been taught and you won't wander far off the path, sweetie. You make sure you stay pure.'

Not that he ever believed her as she grew into a teenager, thought stuff was going on even in school hours, his paranoia ramping up to dangerous levels. That's when he'd really started to show her who was boss, and why she shouldn't step out of line. His belt, his fists, it was all the same to him. All to keep her pure, keep her on the 'straight and narrow'. She wasn't a bad girl, but that didn't seem to matter to her Pop. He thought the worst, whatever she said. It was around then Diana began to dream of another life, of being someone – anyone – else.

Maybe of being a superhero, like the one she shared her name with, dressed in red, blue and gold. From the comics Abi Huston would lend her and she'd devour, hiding them away in her room, imagining what it would be like if she had powers herself. Pop had found a couple once and ripped them up, said they were putting subversive ideas in her head. His weapon of choice that evening: the wooden spoon, careful only to leave welts where nobody would see them – and back in those days folk didn't really care anyway. She had to wonder where God and Jesus fitted into all this, thought that surely *they* wouldn't approve of such behaviour.

Then that day had come, when all of a sudden in class she'd known what Jackie Bishop had been doing over the weekend with Howard Flanagan down in the woods; the kind of things her father was imagining she was getting up to, but wasn't. Nobody was taking the wooden spoon to Jackie, but Diana had also known what would happen in nine months' time. That Jackie would have twins, and have to drop out of school altogether. How she'd known all this – and it had all come to pass, *all* of it – was beyond her, though hadn't her Aunty Glenda who'd visited one time mentioned something about her mother having 'the sight': past and future, Glenda had insisted, her mother had been able to see it all. She hadn't stayed around for long after that, and had never been invited back.

Was that it? Had Diana inherited this ability from her mom? Maybe she did have powers after all, maybe that's what the woman had meant when she said Diana was special. Magical.

If only it had been that simple.

She'd begun noticing it all the time after that, could tell things about people if she concentrated – though it was always strongest at a certain time of the month. Not *that* time, a woman's time, when she'd often catch Pop rooting around in the bathroom bin for evidence that she wasn't like Jackie Bishop. He needn't have worried, Diana was terrified of going anywhere near boys by then…thanks to him.

Not even at the prom, when she'd been asked out by several but had said no to them all – preferring to just go alone, and get picked up by Pop afterwards for the debrief. Of course, he hadn't believed her that nothing had been going on that time either – and it was during his thrashing with the belt that she blurted it out. What she knew about him and the women he saw on his route, the other deliveries he'd been making all these years – good, honest grind – including when her mom had still been alive.

That had made him pause for thought, stand back and gape at her. 'You're just like her,' he'd said then. 'Cursed! You have the Devil inside you, child! Aren't pure, could *never* be pure!'

But it was as he'd come at her that final time she'd realised... Realised how her mom had really met her end, that his attempts to drive out what he thought was a demon had resulted in that woman's premature death; God acting *through* him. Not suicide as the authorities concluded, a hanging, but murder. As Roy saw it, he was releasing his wife – genuinely believed that she was now in Heaven. That he'd sent her there...

Another reason to keep an eye on Diana, in case those tendencies ever surfaced in her, in spite of all his good work. Something else surfaced during that attack, though. Perhaps not all the way, but enough to make her Pop think twice this time – something in her eyes, and in his when he saw it – enough to make him go and fetch his gun instead. Something that definitely wasn't 'pure' as her father always called it.

Diana had escaped, crashed out through the front door – shouldn't have been able to do that, because it was solid wood, locked and bolted – and she just ran. Had no idea where she was going or how she'd even survive, just knowing that anything was better than this. Embarking on another life, away from her Pop.

She'd woken up that first morning, emerging from something of a daze, in someone's barn – her dress shredded in places. Diana had begun crying into her hands and thought she'd never stop. Didn't have a clue who to turn to… Maybe her Aunty Glenda? But she had no idea how to find her – let alone get there. Her father had kept her away from that side of the family, from *every* side of the family come to that.

So, when she couldn't really stay in the barn any longer, Diana set out and started walking. She walked, and walked and walked, up the road as far as she could – was lucky enough to be picked up by a retired couple in their sixties on their way east, who asked questions about the state of her, but didn't push for the answers. Diana ended up staying with them at their place for a few weeks, just to get her head together, but moved on before she started to get too attached.

She figured that a life on the road was the only way to keep a low profile, the only way to avoid the authorities who might be looking for her – who knew what crap Pop had told them about her. Diana got by, more though luck than judgement, working jobs that didn't really need references or even real names – waitressing, handing out flyers, cleaning – like her namesake, she didn't need a man to look after her. She had to be strong, had to learn to survive on her own wits. Telling herself it was better to be alone.

But that hadn't lasted long, and when money dried up and winter would come around, she'd turn to other methods of making a buck. A self-fulfilling prophecy, becoming the very thing that her father always thought she was – being used, but being paid for the privilege; sad sacks she'd tried to block out, tried not to 'read' because it upset her too much.

'Aren't pure, could never *be pure!'*

Retaining control, or so she told herself. Using some of that cash to get good and loaded, even high, at that certain point in the month when she feared she'd become the 'demon' her father had witnessed. Getting by, while all the time dreaming of another life. A better life.

It had gone on like that for years, until she'd met Rick. She'd noticed him at the launderette a few times before, with his basket of clothes that told her he was single. But on this one occasion he'd smiled, said hello, then after a certain amount of initial awkwardness asked her if she wanted to have a coffee with him. Diana had concentrated and attempted a reading, but all she'd got was that he was a nice man. Had the power not been at full strength that day, or had the way she'd felt about him even in those first few moments clouded her judgement? Had the love she'd felt for him later done the same, just like it did with so many other women who didn't even have her abilities? Too blind to see what's right in front of their eyes, or smell it either.

That coffee had turned into a drink, a dinner – a series of dates, then before too long a night back at his place where he'd shown her what it really meant to make love, as opposed to having sex. The closeness two people could feel when they became one. A different kind of magic. Yet not even then did she—

'…like a drink?'

The voice cut in again, and Diana was back in the present. Back with the guy who'd sat on the stool beside her, as he eyed her up and down: taking in the low-cut satin top, the leather skirt and stocking-clad legs. As he asked her if she wanted another vodka. She necked back the drink she had and nodded.

He smiled at her, asked the barman for two and held his glass up for her to clink, which she did. A drink, a dinner, a series of dates and then… No, not this time. And was it her imagination, or did this rube look like Rick as well? The dark hair, the smile.

She was good with faces…

Only because, looking back now, Rick looked like Pop – and how screwed up was that? Should have rung a warning bell right there and then, only it didn't. Was that why she'd done everything in her power to please Rick, to get back that feeling of being wanted which had vanished when her father looked at her a certain way? To try and get back to being safe again…

Once more, the memories intruded. Diana on her wedding day, having used those fake papers to arrange it all – it was surprising the kind of people you got to know on the streets, the contacts you made. She'd only ever lied about that one thing to Rick, her past, and he hadn't pressed her. Said that he didn't need to know all the ins and outs, that whatever she'd gone through it was another life. Not this one, with him.

Funny how the past and the present blur into one, though, isn't it?

They'd only been married a couple of weeks, only just back from the honeymoon actually, when he hit her for the first time. It had been a surprise, definitely, came out of the blue. Some minor disagreement about something, she couldn't even remember what – the shock of it had wiped away all traces – and there it had been, the punch to the stomach that winded her, doubled her over. He'd left her there on the floor of their new apartment, while he went out to have a few drinks with the boys from the firm... Had that been what the argument had been about, Diana not wanting him to go? Wanting Rick to stay with her that Friday night instead? Was that unreasonable? Apparently so...

When he'd returned, smelling of booze, all apologies and horny as anything, she'd told herself that it had all been a misunderstanding. How could she have gotten it so wrong? She couldn't have, her senses told her he was a nice guy.

But, of course, it had happened again. Again and again. The violence, the possessiveness – her not being able to leave the house, while he could do what he liked. Except...except she needed to, at that special time of the month. Needed to get away so that he wouldn't see what she was, especially now she'd cleaned up her act – gone to AA and everything, couldn't use drink or drugs to subdue it. Needed to get away so that Rick didn't realise that she was—

'—*not pure, could* never *be pure!*'

Cursed!

Luckily, it tended to coincide with when he went on his benders – often staying out all night, and telling her he'd been at a pal's house when she knew the truth of it. That he'd been with one of his sluts, cheating – making his deliveries, like Poppa Christmas… The stupid thing was, Diana had put up with it – for *so* long! Her namesake – *both* her namesakes – would have been ashamed of her, but she couldn't see any way out. Only to dream, to hope for another, better life.

That was when fate forced her hand. He'd been waiting for her when she returned one night, sat in the dark smoking – she saw the red tip of his cigarette even before she put the light on.

'Where have you been? It's nearly four in the morning.' Where had *she* been, like he had a right to know – just a husband's right, Diana told herself, but she couldn't even answer him; didn't even know herself, just that she'd had to get away. Not let him, let *anyone* see what her father had seen.

He was rising and striding towards her then, but she was holding up her hands. 'Rick no, please... I'm pregnant.' She'd been waiting to tell him, for the right moment – if there ever was such a thing.

Her words stopped him in his tracks, just as those revelations had done with her Pop so long ago. But if her words had shocked him, then his next ones were just as much of a surprise to her. 'Is it even mine?' he asked.

She was about to yell, about to scream at him: '*Of course* it's yours!' She hadn't been with another man since she'd met Rick, hadn't wanted – let alone needed – to. Then it was too late, because he was already ploughing ahead, intent on finishing what he'd started, probably believing it was someone else's – if it even existed. The punch was harder than ever, right in the stomach again.

And then the baby really didn't exist, would never be carried to term let alone be born. Diana felt the exact moment it happened, because she'd started to develop a bond that surpassed the usual mother and daughter connection. Clutched at her stomach and breathed in heavily, felt all the waste, everything that child ever could have been.

Everything Rick had taken away from her.

Felt that, and felt something else besides. She felt angry… No, *furious*. Diana couldn't hold it back any longer, didn't want to. This was something beyond the usual urges that she escaped to fulfil, so that she didn't hurt anyone unintentionally. Some livestock, woodland creatures – then she was able to rein it back in. Not tonight. Not after this.

She could see it on Rick's face, see it in his eyes – saw the same fear Pop had experienced, only Rick didn't have a gun in the house to fetch. Couldn't stand the things. It wouldn't have stopped her anyway.

Not unless it had been filled with silver bullets.

Then she was on *him* for a change, raking him with her claws, tearing out his throat with her teeth, killing him not for food – but for revenge. Something she should have done long ago. By the time she was finished with Rick, there was very little left. What wasn't splattered all over the walls, the floor and ceiling, she'd chewed and swallowed, savouring the final moments of him. It was why, she often thought to herself later, she'd never been able to get a sense of Rick's future when she sniffed him… Because he didn't have one. She'd seen to that.

A brutal, messy divorce.

Diana hadn't been able to stay after that, not even long enough to gather her things or get any money together – because she could hear the sirens even as she changed back. A concerned neighbour most likely, complaining about the noise. 'Sounds like someone's being murdered in that apartment.' Sort of. Thank Christ she hadn't married Rick under her real name…

So she was on the road again, only this time she had relished it. Freedom, an escape. Yet another life. Alone… She'd found more deadbeat jobs, but never turned to the oldest profession ever again. And she'd learned to embrace this…'curse', what she was; embrace and control it, make it work for her. Do what her mother had never been given the opportunity to.

Only problem was, livestock would no longer satisfy. Not now she'd tasted Rick, tasted human flesh. Not even AA would be able to help her with that one. Which was why she hunted, usually only those who deserved it

– or she thought she was doing a favour. She was too old for clubbing, and hadn't really been into that when she was younger anyway – too busy making ends meet. Dating sites were fertile ground, out of the way bars, Singles Nights…

'…get so lonely sometimes, don't you find that?'

She'd been drifting again, not really taking any notice of what the man was saying to her – so Diana just nodded. It *was* a lonely life, this one she led. Couldn't let anyone else in, not just because of what she was, but because of what they might do to her. She'd had enough of that; no more.

'Yeah, me too. You…you don't look like the kind of woman who needs to hang out at evenings like this one, if you don't mind me saying.' He smiled again with those oh-so-white teeth. Diane sniffed him up now, knowing he couldn't be Pop (that man had taken his own life a few years after she left, she'd heard, blew his brains out…just couldn't handle what he'd married, what he'd spawned). Knowing also it couldn't be Rick, that was impossible. No, this guy – the

- 190 -

doppelgänger – his name was Tatum, and he worked at Lucky Marv's Used Cars.

Treated women as abysmally as her father and husband had, though. There was a string of them behind him, all of whom had fallen foul of his abuse. Maybe not physical, this time, but mental. A game-player. It was just a bonus surely that he looked like Pop, that he looked like Rick.

Well, she had a few games in mind for him.

'That's very kind of you.'

'Not at all. You're...well, you're beautiful...' He waited for a name, but when it wasn't forthcoming he told her his instead – the one she knew already.

'Look, do you want to just blow this place?' Diana said to him. 'It's pretty dead anyway.' *Though not as dead as you'll be soon*, she thought to herself.

'Er...yeah. I mean...if you're sure?' Wasn't used to it being so easy, it had thrown him.

'I'm sure,' Diana told him, a confidence that hadn't been in her voice when she was growing up, nor when she'd been Rick's bitch. 'Let's go.' She noticed him watching as she shuffled forwards on the stool, allowed him a glimpse of the tops of those stockings. Make the most of it, she thought, because I'll have a few more sights to show you before the evening is over.

They grabbed their coats, his a blazer-style jacket as she'd thought, hers a fur – fake, naturally. Then they made their way outside, Tatum holding the door for her like the gentleman he wasn't. Diana cast a look up at the sky, clouds rolling across the full moon.

'You know, this kind of thing doesn't usually happen to me.'

'No?'

'I mean, a woman like you... You're so...'

'Direct?' Diana offered, to help him out.

'Yeah, that's it. Direct. You know your own mind.'

And yours, as well.

'Life's too short to be anything else,' said Diana. 'Don't you think?'

He smiled again, nodded. 'So, where do you want to go? My place? Your place...?'

'What's wrong with right here?' she said.

Tatum swallowed dryly. 'What, here? In the car park?'

Diana looked around, spotted the cameras

trained on the space ahead of them. Shook her head.

'My car, you mean?'

She shook her head again. 'Round the back, there's an alleyway.' Diana knew it all too well, had already scoped it out. Knew it, and others like it – had used them before.

'You're...you're keen, aren't you?' There was a hitch in his voice, and surprise – like he thought it would have taken much more than buying a drink to get her this far. Never in a billion years thought he'd be screwing her behind the back of that very bar twenty minutes later.

'Why wait?' she said to him. 'Life's—'

'Too short, yeah. You said.' He grinned now, nodded. 'Okay, after you then.' Tatum held out his hand, once more pretending to be the gent. But when they got to the alley in question, he started to reveal his true colours. He grabbed Diana and pushed her back against the wall, breath coming in short bursts. Then he was up against her, grinding against her—

Good, honest grind...

She could feel his hardness jabbing into her thigh. His mouth was on hers, hands all over her as if he couldn't decide which bit to explore first.

Diana pushed him off easily.

'What?' he said, genuinely surprised. 'I thought this was what you wanted.'

'Not quite,' Diana said to him.

'So what... Don't tell me you've fucking changed your mind now, because...' He let the sentence tail off, but the inference was clear. Now they were here and in the heat of the moment, he was getting what he wanted whether she liked it or not. None of this was helping his cause.

'Because what?' she pushed. 'What are you going to do about it, if I have?'

Tatum smirked. 'I've already done it,' he told her.

Diana was aware of someone else in the alley with them. Two people in fact, no, three... a couple of them wearing caps. How had she not picked up on that before? Tatum wasn't alone. Wasn't the only one intent on getting what he wanted tonight. How had she not... She took a step, almost lost her balance and had to reach for the wall.

He... the bastard had drugged her. But

how? In the drink? She'd been watching it the whole time, hadn't gone to the head or anything. Besides, stuff like Wayne used wouldn't work on her. So...

'Not feeling great, Diana?' asked Tatum. How the fuck did he know her name? Her *real* name. 'Aww, a pity. That'll be this.' He tapped his lips, then produced a chapstick from his pocket. 'I make it myself, infused with tiny particles of silver. Oh, don't worry, it won't kill you – just slow you down for a little while, long enough to do what we need to.'

Silver? Diana was aware she was frowning again. Not only did he seem to know who she was, *what* she was, but he knew what weakened her.

Weakening her resolve...

This whole thing had been planned, more so than anything Wayne could have come up with. But how? She'd 'read' this guy, smelled Tatum and—

'Now, I know what you're thinking. How could you have got it so wrong? Of course, I'm not Tatum. I don't work on a car lot... But the guy I took this from does.' He produced something else now from his other pocket.

'Just another product in our beauty line. Sweat from one Tatum Jones, sprayed on...' The man who wasn't Tatum demonstrated by pressing the top and Diana got another whiff of the person who was; his past, his future. A mask, a shield. 'It works a treat, totally confuses the target.'

Target? Shit!

The other men were getting closer now and with one sniff she knew who *they* were, just as they knew everything about her. Hunters, professionals belonging to a...a league; people who left nothing to chance. They'd even gone through their ranks to find someone who looked a bit like her father, like Rick – exploiting another one of her vulnerabilities.

They had weapons now, she saw. One held a lethal-looking silver machete, another a large Bowie knife, the final one a small hand-held axe. Quiet weapons that wouldn't draw too much attention. Diana tried to will the change, to bring it on, but it was frustratingly out of reach, like an itch she just couldn't scratch.

'Tatum' stepped forward again. 'You were right about one thing, life *is* short – for you!' Then he punched her in the stomach, doubling her over. The recognisable pain came back to her as she slid down the wall. The pain, the memories again. The hurt, the anger. The loss.

'All right,' said the man, nodding to his companions, 'let's finish this.'

Diana's eyes narrowed, willing the change – even looking up again at the moon for help. And it was as she did so that she saw it, a silhouette actually moving across that silvery circle, like a much hairier E.T. Moving, falling, dropping behind the hunters with a growl.

They turned, but were way too slow for this creature – which towered above them, clawing machete-man out of the way in seconds. He landed against the opposite wall, bones crunching, his weapon clanking to the ground.

There was very little room to manoeuvre in that tight space, and though the hunter with the knife made a lunge, it was easily dodged by this new player in the game. Then suddenly the hand that had been holding the knife was separated from the arm. The man clutched it to his chest, blood pumping blackly from it as he screamed.

'Look…look out!' Diana cried, pointed to the creature's right – where the hunter with the axe was bringing the weapon downwards. Would have embedded in his opponent's head had it not been for the warning. Now, instead, a large paw sunk into the man's chest, pulling him in so that huge teeth could do their worst, biting into his face and tearing most of it away with a wrench of the head.

Fake Tatum backed away, mouth hanging open. He wasn't sure how the tables had turned so quickly, but that wasn't really important right now. He needed to get away, run. Live to fight another day, because life was...

The huge wolf turned its attentions toward him, dropping the axe-man at its feet. It was only now, close-up, that Diana could see the streaks of grey in its fur. The look in its red and yellow eyes... These men weren't the only ones who could disguise their scent.

It was about to lunge, to attack, when Diana shouted: 'No!' The wolf turned towards her, and they locked eyes for the second time that evening. It cocked its head. 'He's mine!'

And now, mustering all her strength, channelling all that hate and fury – Diana changed. She easily matched the other wolf in size, snarling and howling as she rose to her full height.

The man in front of her, the one who looked like her father, her ex, and probably now wished that he didn't, pissed his pants. He tried to get away, but that just made it all the more satisfying for her. The attack was even more ferocious than the one all those years ago that had ended Rick's life.

When she was done, when she finally looked up again – chewing on bits of the final hunter – the other wolf was gone. Vanished, just like he had from the bar. Diana sniffed the air, but of course she couldn't smell him, didn't have a hope of tracking him.

Then she realised why he'd fled. There was no sign of the hunter with the missing hand, he'd got away; the only one who had. She wondered who the stranger was, whether this would now cause trouble for him? It would definitely alert *her* to the fact hunters were on her tail.

She wondered also, if she'd met the stranger earlier on, when she was younger, whether things might have been different. Whether they would have got on, even had a chance at making it – making something... Both the same, shared experiences. Not alone.

Diana shook her head. A fantasy of a better life, a different—

No. Enough. She wouldn't do that anymore. No more dreaming. It was time to go, before the sirens came again. Time to hit the road once more.

Thanks to the stranger, the only man who'd ever been there for her when she needed him, there would be more content, more to fill up her days and years... hopefully.

And for that she would always be grateful.

*

From the rooftop, Neil watched the van drive away.

He would track it, follow the guy with one hand (a familiar move he'd used before, another parallel) and take care of him – but by now he'd almost certainly alerted more of his kind. Neil would be on their radar now, just like she was...the she-wolf back there he'd helped. He didn't like to interfere, and their reputations went before them; if he hadn't believed it then, he did after witnessing the savageness she'd displayed below. The female of the species was most definitely more deadly than the male. Briefly, he wondered what had made her quite that brutal.

She could've taken care of the whole lot of them easily, if that hunter hadn't drugged her. Trap or no trap, she would have polished them off in no time. And he began to think himself, that maybe a companion on this journey, this trip he'd begun after leaving his hometown, might not be such a bad thing after all.

Might not have been a bad thing from the start, if he'd hooked up with one of them instead of hanging around with his mates. Maybe none of the awful things that had occurred would have happened if he'd had someone like her to share life with. To talk to. His friends, his wife, his child…all those different lives, gone. But with her, with the woman back there…

Neil shook his head. It was too late for all that, it had already happened. That had been his fate and his story wasn't over yet. This shit would come back to bite him, he knew that as well; it always did. You reap what you sow. But he'd deal, the same as he always did. Anyway, that was for another time. Another place.

Another life to come.

Story Notes

Nightlife

By the late '90s I'd already tackled those other fundamental horror staples, zombies and vampires, so I figured it was high time I turned my attention to werewolves. Upon approaching this one, I was very conscious of the fact that the subject had been done to death in films and fiction, and I knew that probably even my idea would be similar to something else from the past. One of the ways I got around this was by withholding the fact that it's a werewolf tale until the climax, and this means that when you go back and read it again a lot of the lines have very different meanings.

Half-Life

When I was looking for new material to write to go along with my novellas 'Pain Cages' and 'Signs of Life' for Books of the Dead in 2011, I started thinking about 'Nightlife' – about maybe dropping in and seeing how Neil was doing these days. More and more as my career goes on, I find myself revisiting stories and doing sequels: most recently working on the sequels to *RED* for SST publications, which – along with *The Curse of the Wolf* from Hersham Horror (soon to be reprinted in *More Monsters* published by Black Shuck) – also loosely tie in to Neil's life. And, as I was approaching middle age myself, I thought it might be a good time to comment on that, on lost youth and how the mistakes of the past can sometimes come back and – quite literally in this case – bite you. I had such a good time with this tale, writing about what Stephen Volk (who was introducing *Pain Cages*) called my 'Chav Werewolves', that I started to think about Neil a little later on in his life and maybe tying up the whole thing in a trilogy...

Lifetime

So, we finish the original three stories with an ending, but also a beginning. I'd always wanted to conclude Neil's story, the 'Life Cycle' trilogy as I've named it – so my thanks to Peter and Jan at Alchemy Press for allowing me to do that in the first *Monsters*, and to Steve Shaw for giving it a new lease of life here. This novelette allowed me to imagine what Neil might be like as an old man (I'm not there yet, before you say anything) but also comment on the generation gap as I see it and have experienced it. They say 'youth is wasted on the young', and nowhere is that more apparent than when Neil is attempting to pass the wisdom of his years on to Troy. It's an ending because of how we leave Neil, but it's also the beginning of Troy's story – which brings things round full circle, I think, especially with the final line. They also say, 'the more things change the more they stay the same', and that's a pretty good note upon which to finish that trilogy.

Another Life

But, of course, no story ever truly ends... *The Life Cycle* takes place over such long period of time – a 'Lifetime', in fact – and there's so much which happens in-between, that obviously there's massive scope to fill in some of the gaps. When I was first discussing putting the trilogy together with Steve, I mentioned that at some point I wanted to write a short that takes place between 'Half-life' and 'Lifetime', maybe about one of the female werewolves Neil briefly refers to from his travels (and here I need to thank Peter Coleborn again for asking where all the she-wolves are in this universe; the answer was I was trying to say something about predatory males in the first three tales, but it did get me thinking...). In one of those fortunate misunderstandings that lead to something good, Steve thought I meant I wanted to include it in this book – which actually gave me the impetus to sit down and tell Diana's story. There are obvious parallels to Neil, and I liked the idea of their stories crossing over – if only momentarily – but she's definitely her own woman. And, as I wrote the tale, I got a real sense that, as with Troy, there might be more stories to tell with her at the centre. But that's for the future, as Neil himself says. In another time, another place.

Another life.

Also by Paul Kane:

Novels
Arrowhead (Abaddon, 2008)
Broken Arrow (Abaddon, 2009)
Arrowland (Abaddon, 2010)
Hooded Man (Omnibus) (Abaddon, 2013)
The Gemini Factor (Screaming Dreams, 2010)
Of Darkness and Light (Thunderstorm Books, 2010)
Lunar (Bad Moon Books, 2012)
Sleeper(s) (Crystal Lake Publishing, 2013)
The Rainbow Man (as P.B. Kane) (Rocket Ride Books, 2013)
Blood RED (SST Publications, 2015)
Sherlock Holmes and the Servants of Hell (Solaris Books, 2016)
Before (Grey Matter Press, 2017)

Novellas & Novelettes
Signs of Life (Crystal Serenades, 2005)
The Lazarus Condition (Tasmaniac Publications, 2007)
Dalton Quayle Rides Out (Pendragon Press, 2007)
RED (Skullvines Press, 2008)

Pain Cages (Books of the Dead, 2011)
Creakers (chapbook) (Spectral Press, 2013)
The Curse of the Wolf (Hersham Horror Books, 2014)
Flaming Arrow (Abaddon, 2015)
The P.I.'s Tale (2016)
Snow (Stormblade Productions, 2016)
End of the End (Abaddon, 2016)
The Crimson Mystery (SST, 2016)
The Rot (Horrific Tales, 2016)
Beneath the Surface (with Simon Clark) (SST, 2017)

Collections
Alone (In the Dark) (BJM Press, 2001)
Touching the Flame (Rainfall Books, 2002)
FunnyBones (Creative Guy Publications, 2003)
Peripheral Visions (Creative Guy Publications, 2008)
The Adventures of Dalton Quayle (Mundania Press, 2011)
Shadow Writer (Mansion House Books, 2011)
The Butterfly Man and Other Stories (PS Publishing, 2011)

The Spaces Between (Dark Moon Books, 2013)
Ghosts (Spectral Press, 2013)
Monsters (Alchemy Press, 2015)
The Dead Trilogy (NewCon Press, 2016)
Shadow Casting (SST Publications, 2016)
Nailbiters (as Paul B Kane) (Black Shuck Books, 2017)
Death (The Sinister Horror Company, 2017)
Disexistence (Cycatrix Press, 2017)

Non-Fiction
The Hellraiser Films And Their Legacy (McFarland)
Voices in the Dark (McFarland, 2010)
Shadow Writer – The Non-Fiction. Vol. 1: Reviews (BearManor Media)
Shadow Writer – The Non-Fiction. Vol. 2: Articles & Essays (BearManor Media)

Visit Paul Kane at his website:
www.shadow-writer.co.uk

Now Available and Forthcoming in the Black Shuck Shadows Range:

Shadows 1
    The Spirits of Christmas by Paul Kane
Shadows 2
    Tales of New Mexico by Joseph D'Lacey
Shadows 3
    Unquiet Waters by Thana Niveau
Shadows 5
    The Death of Boys by Gary Fry
Shadows 6
    Broken on the Inside by Phil Sloman
Shadows 7
    The Martledge Variations by Simon Kurt Unsworth

blackshuckbooks.co.uk/shadows

Made in the USA
Columbia, SC
20 June 2018